Praise for *Annaliese, Sound and True*

In the face of the timbering holocaust that swept through the Appalachian Mountains in the early 1900s, Annaliese dares to confront those who would slash every tree. Widow, mother, lumber mill owner, Annaliese discovers her strengths and passion as she thwarts male domination and greed in a heroic fight to save her land and her family. You'll cheer her on every step of the way. A beautiful, evocative book from an important new voice in fiction.

— **Mary Alice Monroe**, *New York Times* bestselling author

Also by Lindy Keane Carter

Annaliese From Off

Annaliese, Sound and True

Lindy Keane Carter

MILLEDGE **&** LUMPKIN
PUBLISHING

MILLEDGE & LUMPKIN
PUBLISHING

Copyright © 2018 by Lindy Keane Carter
www.lindycarter.com

All rights reserved.
Book cover design: Damonza.com
Logo design: Mary Lee Carter
Formatting: Polgarus Studio
Manufactured in the United States of America

ISBN-13: 978-1-7320520-0-0 (paperback)
ISBN-13: 978-1-7320520-1-7 (ebook)

Dedicated to Dellita

Constant light, remarkable friend

1

Two women sat in the porch rockers they occupied every morning and every afternoon. One of them believed they had made peace months ago. The other stared at the road reliving all that had happened.

The problem was, Annaliese Stregal had had too much time to think. When her mind should've been occupied with community and family but wasn't, the memories had circled back like squatters returning to an abandoned acre. The loyal servant beside her mending stockings, she never was at fault, Annaliese reminded herself.

Still.

Annaliese fanned her face with a magazine as she watched neighbor children chase one another in the dirt road that no one had bothered to name and never would. Among its string of unpainted houses, hers was the largest, with two stories and wraparound porch. Though she'd left it unpainted so as to not ruffle feathers, the gleam of money shone from its sheer size nevertheless. Humble daffodils hugged the rock pillars beneath the porch, fruit of the bulbs she had planted herself.

The children stirred up a cloud of red dust with their tagging and wheeling. Annaliese imagined the grit wafting through her windows to settle on clocks, pillows, lamp chimneys, and her beloved books. A wagon rattled by, its driver touching his finger to his hat for the women. The children rushed away from the wheels, then returned when he passed like water flowing back to its bed.

Annaliese wanted to get in that wagon so bad she didn't care where it was going, whether to the town's livery stable a half mile away, or the gristmill on the far side, or Atlanta eighty miles south. But the child growing in her belly chained her to this house. Throughout February, March, and now ten days into April, the neighbor ladies saw her on the porch and sent over knowing waves and comforting sayings such as the sun always shines for an April baby. Annaliese hoped so, but mostly she hoped the sun wouldn't set on the last day of April with no baby delivered. So many things that she loved she hadn't been able to do for months—riding horses, tromping through the forest to find wildflowers, firing her Winchester at tin cans behind her home in the mountains. Sewing and reading were her only entertainment now. No children to keep her busy, for she'd sent them to Louisville to be with her sister and mother for a while. No husband to attend to. No one in the house but Annaliese and the woman beside her.

Two years ago, Annaliese was perfectly happy being idle in the parlors of Louisville, Kentucky. Back then, immersed in scones and tea, she never would've believed the woman she had become in Georgia, this woman with horse-hardened legs and complexion that was no longer a socialite's alabaster. Freckles bloomed in earnest across her wind-chapped cheeks and crow's-feet dug in around her eyes, for in her exuberance she'd pulled off her sunbonnet too often. Men still admired that face, though. Women did, too. Through jealousy's green lens, they studied the delicate jaw holding firm at thirty years of age and the fine-boned cheeks, the strawberry blonde hair swept up into a sloppy, sensual bun. Anyone who took the time to linger on her eyes saw that they were glistening repositories of knowledge, for Annaliese learned things quickly and recalled them easily.

Stuck in the house in town since she'd come down from the mountains in February, she felt like a fossil—cemented to limestone, waiting for deliverance into the sunshine. Once a day, she waddled into town—

waving away the neighbors' fussings from their windows—to fetch the mail at the post office: letters from home, her husband's industry journals, women's magazines, suffragette newsletters, newspapers, catalogues. She devoured them all. Twice sometimes.

Annaliese put the magazine down to pick lint off her black dress and ponder what she could do for the forty-three minutes until today's post office trip. The laundry was folded, the table was set for dinner four hours yet. Her dress jumped. A tiny elbow or heel traveled across her belly, flexed, and resubmerged.

The woman beside Annaliese looked over at the dress moving as if of its own accord and smiled. Ruth Simmons bit off her thread, rolled up the stocking, and dabbed a handkerchief at cheeks marked only by the last of adolescence's pimple storms. She pulled a thin braid the color of a mouse away from her neck and dabbed there, too. Her eyes held knowledge of a different kind, the sum of her eighteen years in the hollows of the Appalachian mountains.

Annaliese pushed her rocker into another round of creaks and shifted her gaze to the mountains that rose in calm undulations into the April sky, each one higher and smokier than the last. From here, the forest looked like a green wash of trees, but she had learned in her two years in Georgia that trees were the least of it.

The forest was a vast universe of organisms, much of it underground. With one good push of a shovel, Ruth had shown Annaliese the fungi roots entwined with the roots of bushes and trees. What they did for each other, Ruth couldn't say, but for certain something important was being shared, she felt. When you injured one, the other did poorly, she said. After that, Annaliese viewed the jaunty caps of mushrooms as but a hint of many relationships below. She pictured the forest soils being held together by miles and of miles of roots, springtails, beetles, worms, and other busy creatures almost too small to see. Now she knew that soil came from many left-behinds—the dust of rocks imperceptibly split apart by tree roots, decaying trees and leaves, animal scat, beetle shells, the hair of deer mice.

Annaliese and her two children could identify tree species by their leaves and bark—the eastern hemlock, yellow birch, American chestnut, chestnut oak, red maple, white pine, red oak, and the granddaddy of them all, the towering tulip poplar, tallest hardwood tree in North America. Every March save the last, they combed the woods for serviceberries, one of the first signs of spring, so named by the mountaineers because when the berries busted out, the circuit-riding preacher would be along soon. Now, in full-blown spring, Annaliese pictured the wildflowers rising from the waking earth in their waves of yellow cups, white stars, pink slippers, crimson hearts. The homely squawroot was being eaten to the ground by bears still gorging. Plants were pushing through leaf litter to feed the voles, deer, and turtles. Every life depended on others in the primeval layer of ground, every creature contributed to the balance. She was missing it all.

But dark forces were at work in those hills too.

Timber speculators, timber brokers, and loggers slamming through the forests. Desperate men and their axes. That delicate universe would never fully recover from the timber holocaust now sweeping through the Appalachian mountains. She recalled the day her husband, John, came home to announce that he was abandoning his law practice to start a lumber business with his brother in Georgia. For days they argued. He never did give her one good reason why he would leave behind a thriving business, saying only that she'd see. Trust me, he said.

When they arrived in 1901, Annaliese and her sister-in-law, Lucenia, didn't immediately understand the effect that logging had on every living thing. They were just trying to feed everyone, keep their four children safe, build a schoolhouse, hire a teacher. It didn't take them long, though, to see the company's damage on every bludgeoned slope, in every bloodied river. They decided to replant one hundred clear-cut acres of Black Face Mountain with bareroot pine seedlings. They called it their suffragette project—John called it their suffragette shit—but Lucenia didn't live long enough to see the seedlings go into the ground. Annaliese made sure they did in time to survive the winter of 1902-03 and when the weather allowed, she rode up to Black Face to check on them. In February, Ruth made her stop riding horses. Last time she saw the seedlings, they were green and growing but vulnerable.

Upstairs in Annaliese's bedroom, her wedding photograph sat on a bureau. Sometimes in the five months since John's death, she covered it with a pillow and buried her face there, screaming at him for leaving her with two—almost three—children, seventeen thousand acres, a lumber company to figure out what to do with, and a toxic legacy with Ruth still playing out. She couldn't sell the company. She couldn't run it by herself. She couldn't go back to Louisville. So many messes he'd left for her to clean up. So many reasons to scream.

2

Henry Chastain pushed away from the desk where he wasn't getting any work done and went to his office doorway. For the fifth time since breakfast, he looked down the wooden boardwalk that ran in front of the establishments of Pinch, Georgia. People hurried in and out of stores, baskets and bulging sacks in hand. None of them were coming for him with news. Only two even looked at him. Across the main road—a clay avenue lined with wheel ruts made on wetter days but now as hard as flint under the cloudless April sky—the windows of the Gilmer County Bank and Smith's Mercantile struggled under veils of red dust. He watched two women wipe the window at Smith's to look over Mrs. Smith's disturbing millinery display—five hats of riotous feathers and ribbons hanging broken necked on headless poles.

He sat down again to try to write a persuasive closing argument for next week's trial, another lawsuit from a farmer, the plaintiff he dreaded the most. He looked at his calendar with the court date circled in thick pencil: April 17, 1903. Henry hated arguing that a farmer should be denied compensation for the cow or mule that the Atlanta, Knoxville and Northern Railroad had mowed down, but the railroad wrote Henry's paychecks. So he would summon a professional demeanor to watch the plaintiff in his droopy overalls explain to a jury of twelve white men he'd known all of his life how it was that the cow or mule had come to be on the loose, the degree of carelessness being the deciding factor when the jury was assigning fault.

Henry's people weren't farmers, they were preachers, but everyone in the mountains knew the grind of farming, the agony of waiting all year to have maybe two hundred in cash when the crops came in, if they came in. A dead mule could mean the end of the farm.

Far as Henry could tell, preaching had never called him, so he could honestly tell his father he hadn't missed the call. No question he'd inherited the family oratory skills—people hung on every word of his stories—but he preferred a dinner party as his audience. He couldn't see himself in a pulpit. All that outrage, all of those dire warnings. Growing up in a valley cabin near Pinch, Henry came to town as everyone else did for the year's best entertainment: the week of civil trials in May and the criminal trials in October. Standing his ground against the pushing and shoving outside the courtroom's open window, Henry got hooked on the drama. At fourteen, he decided that the courtroom was the pulpit for him. His father said he wouldn't support that as all lawyers were liars. This was an impotent threat since his father had little support, monetary or otherwise, to withhold. At eighteen, Henry borrowed *Blackstone's Commentaries, Cobb's Digest,* and other textbooks from visiting attorneys. At a session of the Superior Court in the Pinch courthouse, Henry asked to be examined for admission to an apprenticeship. The judge quizzed the sweating, earnest teenager and, with a smile, waved him on to his next hurdle.

Henry traveled through two counties to ask a revered attorney to take him on. The portly barrister, an elderly man fond of cigars, fruit cobblers, and fried chicken livers, ran his runny eyes up and down the skinny kid and asked if he was Republican or Democrat. Henry knew there was only one right answer in north Georgia, but he was too open-minded to align with either camp. Baptist, he finally came up with. The attorney said that that was all right, too. One dollar a day and you can sleep in the room behind the office, the old man said.

For five years, Henry filed motions at the courthouse, dug up legal precedents, set up trial dates, contacted the other attorneys involved, and watched the old master argue cases in court. When he had scant evidence with which to build a defense, he ramped up the histrionics. The more volume and high-faluting language, the better. As these theatrics swayed a jury more often than not, Henry took note that outrage and dire warnings had their place in his life after all.

When knocks came at the office door in the middle of the night, it was Henry who opened it to listen to someone's heated charges of an assault at a fish fry or poker game. Off he would trudge with the aggrieved party to locate the attacker, only to find when they got there that the aggrieved had cooled down and no longer wanted to press charges. Henry got the best education a budding lawyer could hope for. He wrapped up knife wounds, broke up fights, and held the bastard babies of mothers defending their virtue on the witness stand. Clients, he learned, could be more slippery than the opposing side. He learned how to worm the truth out of the squint-eyed to discover who, in fact, had hornswoggled whom.

Returning to Pinch to hang out his shingle, Henry defended and prosecuted cases of many kinds, but there was nothing he could do for a farmer when a bank foreclosed on his farm. Some days, Henry looked up from his desk to see another one leaving the bank with defeated shoulders, hat held at his side in work-roughened hands, suddenly adrift and unsteady on his feet.

In the spring of 1900, precisely three years earlier, a man walked into his office looking for help with investigating the tax titles and deeds of hundreds of land parcels. John Stregal, a Louisville attorney, was buying land and wanted no lawsuits over titles, a notorious mess in north Georgia with family disputes, squatters' rights, sloppy filing of land grants at the courthouse (if anyone had filed at all), and the mishmash of Georgia law. Henry sized him up as a principled man, as principled as a lumber mill owner could be, and Henry needed the work. To his surprise, they became friends. When John's wife and two children arrived in the spring of 1901, John swept the bachelor into their holidays and dinners at their home near the sawmill in the mountains. Now, with John gone, Henry was trying to take care of his friend's wife who was about to give birth, but he had to be careful. She was a beautiful woman, and wealthy. Tongues in Pinch wagged over her every move. Responsibility for her weighed heavily in Henry's heart, right beside other feelings that he couldn't act upon. Yet.

Henry scrawled a few sentences for the closing argument, deemed them as exciting as a boiled egg, and put his pen down. The sound of footsteps coming hard on the boardwalk brought him out of his chair again.

Henry recognized the man in the doorway as one of Annaliese's neighbors. "The baby's a'comin'," the man said. "Herschel sent me. Call the doctor yonder in Atlanta." He pointed at the telephone on the wall, one of three in town, as though Henry needed reminding where it was.

When Henry hung up, he said, "They said they'll try to get him on the next train up here."

"Three or four hours then. Hope he gets here in time," the man said, helping himself to a chair.

"Ruth is with her, right?"

"Yep."

Outside, someone rolled a barrel down the sidewalk. A horse neighed, wagons rattled, people cursed at one another.

The neighbor rested his forearms on his knees, still trying to catch his breath.

"Water?" Henry asked.

"Don't mind if I do."

As Henry poured water into a glass on the credenza behind him, he heard the man say, "Sure is sad for a woman to have a baby jest a few months after buryin' her husband."

Henry nodded, pushed the glass toward the man.

"You was there when he died, wasn't you? Heard you was there beside her when Mr. Stregal died in the sawmill."

Henry's temples began to throb.

"Terrible what happened," the man said. "Terrible for y'all to see that." He took a sip. "Up close, wasn't you?" he asked. "I heard."

Henry went back to the doorway.

3

Throughout the last hour of her labor, the doctor kept up a stream of talk from his stool at her feet, telling her about the baby's good and steady descent, his surprise at being summoned from Atlanta to these hills, his first sight of the baby's head, the gossip he'd heard on the train, the crowning of the head, when to push, wait, push, the odd names being given to babies lately, when the head was delivered, the shoulders, the baby. Then—silence.

Annaliese collapsed on her pillow. She heard instruments clinking on a metal tray, the croaky cries of her newborn. The seconds were years. Ruth helped her back up to see, but the doctor had the baby angled down in one hand to suction its nose and mouth. Look up at me, thought Annaliese. Say girl, say boy, say congratulations, something!

The doctor kept his face to himself during his attentions to the child, unhurried at least. Finally, he lifted the blanketed baby to Ruth. As she took the bundle, joy drained from her face.

"Ruth?" Annaliese said, reaching for the baby.

The doctor went to the washbowl.

Ruth stared at the newborn as she lowered the child into her mother's arms.

Annaliese's arms went to ice. The baby's mouth. Mangled. The child's upper lip was cleaved as if by a strand of hair running from lip to nose, creating two bulging lumps. A wedge of glistening pink gum lay exposed between them. One nostril was askew. The bottom lip was cruelly perfect—smooth, plump and symmetrical.

"Mrs. Stregal," the doctor said on his way back to the bed after he'd scrubbed his hands and arms.

Annaliese yanked the blanket off and ran her hands over the sticky body, from the splayed arms to the doughy feet. Deaf to the infant's startled cries, she pushed apart the knees, noted the cleft of her sex, rotated her legs, closed them, counted fingers and toes. She turned her over, ran trembling fingers along the spine, then the head. Annaliese turned her back. The mouth shocked her all over again. She cupped the head in her hands and stared at the mouth. "What—how—what happened to her?" she cried.

"Usually, it's poor diet, ma'am," the doctor said. "But in your case, well, that's not likely. Tell you the truth, we just don't know."

"But she can feed, right?" Ruth asked. "I seen older children, men, and women with a mouth like this, so they do grow up. You can feed them." She looked over at the doctor. "Ain't that so?"

"But this baby also has a cleft palate," he said.

"A what?" Ruth asked

"The roof of her mouth has a hole in it," he said.

Ruth dared a look at the stricken face at her elbow.

"She can't suck," he said.

"But there must be special bottles, special nipples surely," Annaliese said as she tightened the blanket around the baby, blinking into the storm above her.

"You can try to feed her from a cup." The doctor put his hand on Annaliese's shoulder.

"Try to?"

"I'll be honest, ma'am, it's hard work to get enough milk in babies like this. Sometimes, the milk comes out their nose, they panic, gag, tire, give up. But it's possible."

Annaliese pushed his hand away. "What about surgery?"

The doctor took a deep breath. It was clear to him from the voluptuous rugs downstairs and the fact that this woman had sent for an Atlanta doctor that she could pay for surgeries—indeed there would be several—but money wasn't the worry. "Surgeons won't operate on a baby before ten pounds. I'd say she's got about four to go," he said.

"We'll get her there. Won't we, Ruth? With your milk and mine?" Annaliese stared at Ruth.

Another infant's cries floated up the stairs, Ruth's four-month-old who drained every drop from her anemic teats every three hours. Ruth crossed her arms across the two wet spots blooming on her blouse and said nothing.

Annaliese stroked her baby's head and her perfect ears, the skin so impossibly soft it barely registered on her fingers, the eyes astonishingly curious so fresh from the womb. When she stroked the cheek, the baby turned toward her breast. The bottom lip moved up and down, ready to latch on, while the gnarled lip above barely moved. "What do I do?" Annaliese managed to ask before sobs choked her.

"Let's get y'all cleaned up," the doctor said. "I need some warm water, fresh linens. Then we'll put her to the breast, stimulate your milk."

"I'll fetch 'em, Miss Anna." Ruth kissed the baby's head and hurried out.

"You know how to express milk?" the doctor asked. "You did that with your other babies?"

Tears rolled down Annaliese's cheeks. "Yes."

He pulled out a handkerchief and handed it to her.

"Into a cup," she said.

"That's right. You'll give her sips."

"Never seen such a thing for a newborn."

"She can do it. Little sips."

More hot tears streamed down her face. Annaliese rushed the handkerchief to her eyes.

"Mrs. Stregal, listen. You'll take your time. Not too much milk or it'll come out her nose." The doctor walked to the foot of the bed to check her bleeding and replaced the crimson-stained cloths between her legs. Moving to the window, he looked down on the neighbors' houses the color of ash, their broom-swept dirt yards. Above the treetops coated with red dust, as everything in this town seemed to be, the second stories of buildings appeared. Beyond it all, the indigo outlines of the ancient Appalachian mountains rose and fell. Cloud shadows slid across their flanks like enormous wet spots on the move. He had never heard of this town in north Georgia, was surprised at the odd name on his train ticket. Pinch, Georgia. He was practically to the border of Tennessee, a mighty isolated place for this woman and this baby.

A distant clock's chimes floated into the room, low and somber. One, two, three. The crying downstairs had stopped. Cupboard doors were being opened and closed.

Annaliese wiped away her tears and lowered the baby to her lap to find something familiar in the features, as was her habit with her newborns—a trace of John, perhaps, or their son or other daughter. Maybe the eyes, were they John's? The nose? But it was askew, so it was hard to tell. The mouth overwhelmed the face, as though that one central distorted feature of the landscape rendered her blind to all else that was surely there. She held her hand above the mouth to eliminate that distraction, but found no trace of anyone. John would've said that Georgia Ann—the girl name they'd chosen—looks like Georgia Ann.

Every muscle, tendon, and ligament below her belly throbbed with pain. She inched back down into her pillow and tucked the baby beside her, this new life so helpless and tentative.

4

Ruth lifted her baby out of her husband's arms and sat down at the kitchen table. Unbuttoning her blouse, she glanced over at the kettle he'd started on the stove and felt that Lucy's nappy was dry. She smiled at him despite the stench that meant he'd burned her biscuits. Sunlight streamed through gauzy yellow curtains dancing on a cottony breeze. A pair of flies rode it in and split off to begin their intrusions.

"Well?" Herschel Simmons asked. His blue eyes searched her troubled face.

"A girl," Ruth said, bringing her baby's eager mouth toward her nipple.

"Miss Annaliese all right?"

"Yes." Ruth gazed at the tiny, perfect, efficient lips getting to work. "But the baby."

Herschel lowered himself into a chair.

"A harelip," Ruth said.

"Lord A'mighty." He shook his scruffy red head. "That child's goin' to have a rough road."

"If she lives."

Herschel looked at his wife.

She told him what was else wrong with the baby.

Herschel squinted. "You ever seen anybody feed a newborn from a cup?"

Ruth shook her head. "Reckon the doctor knows what he's talkin' about though."

He touched the fingertips of his wife's free hand, closed his eyes as did she, and they prayed. At Herschel's "Amen," Ruth opened her eyes. The baby watched them and smiled, breaking the seal, and before she could reclaim it her mother switched her to the other nipple. "Gotta hurry up, Lucy," Ruth said. The baby burrowed in. Ruth looked up at her husband. "Better get on over to Mr. Henry's office, let him know about the baby," Ruth said.

"Hit don't make no sense." Herschel smoothed his freckled hand across the table, found a few grains of salt, and brushed them off onto his overalls. "A son and a daughter already born to her, not a thing wrong with 'em."

"Far as we can see."

"What do you mean?"

"Mr. John. He looked like nothin' was wrong with him, too."

Herschel sat back. "Sure enough."

Steam sputtered from the throat of the iron kettle. Herschel snatched up a dishrag and moved it to the sink where a second kettle sat under the spout of a cast iron pump. He pumped fresh water in and put that kettle on the stove. Soft, smacking sounds from his daughter sweetened the apricot air, a contented sound so full of meaning now to a young man who rarely gave himself over to reflection. Growing up the oldest son of a hard-drinking man who was good at spitting tobacco with bragging-rights accuracy but not at providing for the family of nine, Herschel was the one who chased after dinner through the mountains. Existence, in his experience, depended on what you could seize from one raw moment to the next, be it a brook trout gliding by or a mink whose fur would get you cash money. There was no time for contentment. But then he found Ruth.

At nineteen, he spotted her on the women's side of the Freewill Baptist Church, a sparrow of a girl with a wispy brown braid. He liked the way she looked back at him all serious and reverent but playful too, somehow, with those wiggling eyebrows. After services, he courted her on the church grounds as best he could with all of the kinfolk eyes at work. He found her to be cheerful and God-fearing, but sassy enough to hint at some heat if he ever got that dress off. He didn't. Behind a pine tree, he proposed. She was sixteen and said yes if he'd agree to a six-month engagement, likely what her parents would want. Her family was so poor her father stole corn out of neighbors' fields and took hams from their smokehouses, but nobody wanted to catch the man. Herschel knew that starving or not, her father had his dignity and only one daughter, so Herschel prepared himself for the wait. Over those six months, as she let out her skirt hem a few inches every two weeks as was the custom, Herschel thought he'd go crazy. When her skirt swept the ground, everyone knew they were engaged. Finally, they got hitched and Herschel got his wedding night. Over the two years of their marriage, he'd found that he'd chosen a good wife.

The second kettle was boiling. He picked it up and went back to Ruth, ready to go with her upstairs. The baby's eyelids were halfway down, her mouth barely hanging on to the nipple.

"Did you make the cotton root bark tea?" Ruth asked.

He looked at her, confused.

"Helps stop her floodin' after the birth, remember?" Ruth nodded toward a cabinet.

Herschel pulled down a brilliant green metal canister and pinched up several pieces of bark that he dropped into a teacup rimmed with pink rosebuds.

Ruth put the baby in a basket near the icebox. She looped her arm through the handle of a bag of bed linens, picked up the teacup, and headed upstairs, followed by Herschel with the two kettles.

5

Annaliese rolled onto her other side to let Ruth pull off the sheet and start a fresh one. The doctor held the baby and watched. Finally, when all the smoothing and pillow plumping was done, he lowered her into Annaliese's arms. Ruth handed Annaliese a small cup of water.

"Just a little bit," the doctor said.

A drop slid into the baby's mouth, then several more that weren't supposed to, sending her to gagging and spewing water from her nose. Annaliese got her wiped down and tried again. Again too much flowed past the pulpy lips. Georgia Ann gagged, choked, gulped for breath.

"Your hands are shaking too much," the doctor said.

Annaliese tried again, getting two drops in, then two more.

"Good," he said. "Water's enough for now, until your milk comes in."

"I'll never get enough in her," Annaliese cried.

The doctor inhaled and exhaled slowly.

"We just started tryin', Miss Annaliese," Ruth said.

A train whistle floated in from the depot a mile away. "That the last train south today?" the doctor asked.

"Naw," Ruth said. "There's another one at six."

"Wouldn't want to chance missing it," the doctor said as he latched his black bag closed. "You'll be fine, Mrs. Stregal. Bleeding's stopped. Stay in bed. That young man downstairs, he could give me a ride?"

The women's eyes went hard and they stared at him for heading for the door just like that, arm extended toward the knob, coattails sucking all hope out of the room as they disappeared into the hall. A few minutes later, Herschel's wagon pulled away.

A shaft of afternoon sun sliced low and level into the room, illuminating the baby's swollen little eyes, her clenched fists, the tragic mouth.

"We need to go home," Annaliese said.

"What?"

"Back to Louisville."

"Thought this was your home now."

"This place is cursed," Annaliese cried. "Look at all that's happened to me since I came here to this godforsaken wilderness."

Ruth fell quiet at the blasphemy.

"First my sister-in-law dies, then her husband and John. All three of them gone, leaving me—the one who never wanted to come here—alone."

"The children are right happy here," Ruth said.

"Now this." Annaliese kissed the top of the baby's head. "I need to get home, get her to a Louisville surgeon. What does that Atlanta doctor know? Ten pounds nothing."

"You two ain't gettin' on no train any time soon."

"My family will take care of us."

"We got to get her fed, Miss Anna. Today."

The baby turned toward her mother's breast. Annaliese unbuttoned her nightgown, put the baby to nipple, pushed it in and up. Tears welled in her eyes as the baby tried to latch on with her impossible lips.

"Good girl," Ruth said. "Get Mama's milk to come in."

"Let's try the cup again, but not water. Think you could get some milk of yours into this cup?"

Ruth brought her hand to her neck. "I just fed Lucy. She took it all."

"You could try." Annaliese gave her a long hard look.

"Ain't nothin' there, I'm tellin' you." She poured water into the cup and held it in front of her. "Doctor said water is fine for now. By tomorrow, your milk will come in."

"What if I don't make enough? Then what are you going to do?"

Ruth gasped. "Miss Annaliese, don't be doin' this right now. This is our past talkin', ain't it?" She put the cup in Annaliese's hand. "Ain't you and I had enough pain?"

"Water then." Annaliese put the cup to the baby's lips again. "For now."

6

Fannin County, Georgia

Forty five miles away, a man stood on a bluff looking up the Camp River that was rising fast with the sum of April's rains that lumber mill owners all over north Georgia were counting on. Buck Dawson felt his heartbeat in his throat while he judged whether the river had peaked. He turned to check on his men downstream and the long log that stuck fifteen feet into the river bend. Throughout the fall and winter, the log—an anchored boom that his crew built months ago—had snagged logs sent downstream by Dawson's stumpers and diverted them into a loosely woven cage, the splash dam. Now, the splash dam held hundreds of oak, chestnut, and poplar trees, bouncing into one another like penned cattle. The rising water lapped over its top and surged through the weave. On the riverbank, a dozen men poked peaveys under logs to pry them out from rocks and get them into the splash dam. Along the dam's base thirty feet below, two Negro men frantically tied the last of their dynamite bundles onto stakes.

Dawson heard the brawling waters getting even louder. He turned, decided the water was right, checked on his horse's reins tied to a tree.

"Now!" he shouted down to the men at the base of the splash dam. "Yonder it comes!"

At Dawson's shout, the men with peaveys climbed up the bank.

"Damn it! Blow the splash!" Dawson yelled.

The Negroes got their matches going and ran along the row of bundles, lighting wicks as they went.

"Ten, nine, eight," Dawson yelled, not that anyone could hear.

With their own count pounding in their temples, the two men made it to the creek bank.

A tower of splintered logs tore into the sky. The roar rattled off the canyon walls. Birds shot out of quaking trees. The massive logs in the splash dam lurched back into the river in time to be swept into the churning flood. Small trees along the banks were ripped into the deafening storm, leaving holes that bled in copper-colored rivulets.

Dawson's horse knocked him down with her scrambling, but her reins held fast to the tree. One of the Negroes who still had the stink of nitroglycerine on their hands had gotten far enough away. The other lay writhing on the creek bank, one leg under a log. The crew rushed to him, pried it off with their poles. Even from his distance, Dawson could see the leg's nauseating angle. The cracks and thuds of the logs racing down the river buried the man's screams, nearly three hundred thousand board feet barreling toward Dawson's millpond and sawmill. Dawson knew he'd lose hundreds of trees along the way, some rammed too high on banks and others stuck on rocks.

Just like he knew he'd lose some men. Cost of business.

When he turned back to his horse, he met the cold eye of a rifle.

"You be the lowest man ever lived," the tobacco-roughened voice said. The man shoved the rifle into Dawson's chest.

"Go to hell, Wilkins," Dawson said, straightening to his six foot two.

"Runnin' off game, killin' the fish. How's a man to feed his family?"

"This ain't your land." Dawson pushed the barrel aside.

"Ain't yours neither."

"I have every right to use this river."

"Like hell you do. A bloody mess now for miles."

"You best be runnin' along to tend that still of yours." Dawson smiled, revealing a collision of amber teeth buried in purple gums.

The man's eyes hardened. "I ain't got no still."

"Sure you do. Down there on Mockingbird Creek."

The man spit on the ground.

"Would hate for the revenue officers to find it." Dawson ran his hand over his bald head and down the back of his neck, picking, picking into the fold of skin. He flicked a tick in the mountaineer's direction. With a grin, Dawson slapped his hat back onto his head.

A rail-thin man climbed the slope to get to Dawson, hand ready at the revolver hanging from his belt. He wore a gray homespun shirt stained at the pits and leather galluses hooked to baggy pants. The brim of his lumpy hat shaded his eyes so completely they were barely visible, but in his stride the mountaineer could see menace clearly enough. "What's goin' on?" the man called.

"Wilkins was jest leavin'," Dawson said.

The mountaineer disappeared into a rhododendron thicket.

Dawson mounted his horse and handed his worker a wad of bills. "Take care of that injured man best you can," he said over his shoulder. "I'm heading east to Rabun County."

"Rabun? That's three days away on horse."

"You know a better way to get there, Pickens?"

"Naw, sir. See you later, I reckon," Pickens said.

Dawson gave the horse her head, and as she inched down the slope, limbs and branches flew at them from all directions. At the bottom, he pulled the antsy horse across a stream lined with alders and willows. On the other side, they climbed a hill choked with mountain laurel that eventually thinned at the crest. Dawson looked out across the mountains that rose and fell in lush, green waves before him. He spotted his landmark, a grassy bald he knew to be halfway to Rabun County.

They descended into an old-growth forest of towering trees that gave Dawson hope for finding the giants he sought, the tulip poplar and the chestnut, the only sellable timber at the moment. As the restless land began another sweep toward the sky, the stands of pines and hickory, five to seven feet wide but worthless, shut out the sky. The grade became so steep Dawson had to dismount again. With each step, the horse's grunts grew louder and Dawson's lungs screamed for more oxygen in the thin air. Finally, they reached the top and he pulled out binoculars.

Waves of butchered land rolled away for as far as he could see. Stumps as wide as wagons dotted the hillside, fresh stumps, still bleached and creamy. Poplars, he thought. Young trees stood broken and bent into sure death. Jagged limbs lay strewn across the land upon which they had cast their shade. Dawson guessed that the oxen and wagons had been there in between the rains of the last week. Fresh copper-colored mud oozed from the pulpy earth. For a long while, he stood there letting his lungs and his temper settle down over being beaten to the poplars, but the sun was sinking behind a distant ridge, so he had to move on. Dawson scanned the land again looking for something else. When the last of the day's light had ignited the sky with pink and blue and whippoorwill calls floated through the cooling air, he saw it: a thin plume of smoke rising from a chimney, giving him hope that the people stoking that fire would board him for the night.

Five gawking little girls hung on the man who opened the cabin door. Dawson removed his hat, held it at his side with practiced humility. The man said he could sleep in the barn, and if he'd help his wife catch a chicken, there'd be enough dinner for him.

Dawson led his horse to the barn, got her wiped down and dried, removed the cloth ear covers he'd made to fend off horseflies, and scratched the ears until her eyes closed. He told her tomorrow was another long, tough ride, but she would have fresh hay in a warm stable waiting for her at the end. Soon her nose was in the feed sack, and he was snapping the neck of the slowest chicken in the family's yard. Before he headed in with it, he pulled a gift for the family out of his saddlebag, a Bible, the King James Version. The authentic version. Every word of it.

7

Ruth answered the knock on the front door and found Henry shifting foot to foot, ham in one hand and a basket of biscuits in the other.

"Mr. Henry, Lord, it's good to see you," Ruth said. Dark circles hung under her eyes. "Come on in."

"No, not now. I just wanted to bring this over, see how it's going."

Ruth stepped onto the porch and rubbed her eyes. "Three days of water and a little milk I could manage to get out. Miss Annaliese's milk come in this mornin' but it ain't much."

Henry said, "Can't you give the baby more of yours?"

Ruth reached for the ham. "I got my own young 'un, you know."

"Is it too soon to wean her?"

"At four months? Yes, sir, it is." Ruth's voice had an edge Henry had never heard before.

"I know you're doing all you can, Ruth."

"Yes, sir."

"Please tell Mrs. Stregal I stopped by."

Ruth nodded as she took the biscuits. "Thank you for calling her family when the baby came. Could you do us another favor?" She went down the hall to a table and came back with a letter. "Mail this? It's a letter to the bishop in Savannah asking him to send a priest this a'way to baptize the baby."

"That'll take months."

"Yes, sir, she knows."

"I'll check on y'all again tomorrow." Henry walked down the steps and opened the fence gate.

Henry's horse knew better than he did the best way to get through the trees, so he held the reins lightly. Leaf buds swelled from every branch, and every branch seemed to hold a bird sending its call into the fluttering leaves. Towering chestnut trees spread their limbs toward one another, creating a carpet of dappled sunshine on the forest floor. At the foot of an oak, white bluets twinkled across the roots like strewn stars. The horse passed the beech tree that bore initials carved by Henry's ten-year-old hands, a crusty black *HC* on the silver skin. Skeins of trails began to appear in the forest and joined his, the path that on Sundays delivered families to Shiloh Baptist Church. Its grounds were empty as he approached. A rude church, with metal roof and rugged steps at the front door, rose from the forest duff. Shutters at three windows were open above an apron of red-mud stain along the unpainted boards.

Henry walked up the steps his grandfather had hewn from chestnut logs, each step worn down in the middle. He opened the door that he couldn't remember ever being locked. A gray-haired man looked up from his hammering on a long bench in front of the pulpit.

"Mornin', Pa," Henry said as he walked through three slices of light streaming in the windows.

"Son," the man said, straightening up.

"Looks like the mourners' bench has seen some use." Henry spotted a split in the ten-foot bench. An augur lay on the floor.

The man nodded. "Tryin' to hold it together with a peg here and there."

"Everything else still holdin' up all right?"

"Not really. I reckon it's been a while since you was here." The older man released his words slowly, each one leaden with history.

"Well, that didn't take long," Henry said as he sat down in the first pew.

The man went back to his hammering. "You come from preachers, son. You cain't even come to services?"

"Can't stand the bickering, Pa."

"Some things is worth bickering over. True believers don't hold with these fool notions that ain't true to the Bible."

"Y'all still arguing about the washing of feet?"

The hammer moved on to another peg. "We ain't called hard-shell Baptists for nothin'."

"Heard a group split off, joined up with the Cherry Log faction."

The man pointed his hammer at Henry. "We won't be recognizing their ordinations and baptisms, I'll tell you that. Durn slab offs."

Henry tapped his hand on the back of the pew and looked around at the walls of oak, every inch of them rendered as dull as eggshells by insistent hands with rags. Even the caramel-colored patterns of the oak pews gave off only meager warmth. The floor, the unceiled rafters, the pulpit—all of it was plain, dead, dull, Henry thought. Not so much as a woven cornhusk mat was allowed to adorn the floor.

Henry pointed to the auger. "Need some help with that?" he asked.

"Naw. I'll finish this later. We'd best be gettin' on while we got the day ahead of us." The man picked up his hat. "Horse is out back."

Laying the reins on the horses' necks on the left then the right to manuever through the forest's understory, they climbed the slope that rose hard into the sky and dove hard to the river gorge. The thwack of axes and moans of oxen floated in from a distant slope.

Eventually, they came to a clearing studded with fresh stumps. The foundation of a cabin, with two rough-hewn sills atop on its longest sides, sat surrounded by logs. The older man looked up at the sky. "Looks like we got about four hours. Got to hump it if we're goin' to get them sleepers hewed and notched today."

They rolled an oak log out of a pile and lifted it onto four small blocks, tucking two wedges under each end. The old man took a wooden box out of his pocket, pushed a coiled string around in the crushed charcoal, and handed one end of it to his son. Standing at opposite ends, they pulled the string tight and twanged it against the bark.

"Now we'll make the next line six inches over. Good strong floor beam's got to be six inches square," the old man said.

Henry moved the string and after another twang, he straightened up to look at the two lines, straight and clear along the top of the log.

"Now, you're going to score it," the older man said as he picked up two broadaxes. "Every two or three inches or so."

As a child, Henry had seen his uncles swing the heavy iron head of the broadaxe in one effortless motion, up, down, up, so he lifted the axe with confidence and swung hard into the log's side. The axe got stuck halfway to the charcoal guideline.

"Gotta put more muscle than that into it!" his father said with a laugh. At the other end of the log, he swung his axe into the bark with ease, bringing the blade right up to the black line. He yanked it out and, with the fluidity of a man half his age, slammed it again to sink no deeper than he intended, this time two inches farther down the log from the first score.

Henry wiped his brow with his forearm and took another swing. His father came over to look. "Ain't too bad. You'll get it," he said, pounding him on the back with more energy than Henry appreciated. Ten minutes later, when Henry had made five scores and the old man had made twelve, they started chipping at the scored chunks. When those had fallen away, they stepped back to admire two straight sides, straight as train rails. Two more to go.

Father and son sat down for a drink from their canteens.

"This is goin' to take forever," Henry said.

"Cabin this size, twenty-four feet long, 'bout six to eight months. You in a hurry?"

"Guess not."

"You ain't never goin' to live here, are you?"

Henry shrugged. "Who knows?"

"The way them loggers are takin' down trees all 'round us, ain't goin' to be no decent place to live anyhow."

"I know."

"Cain't you do somethin' about this loggin' with your lawyerin'?"

"Market forces at work, Pa. It's all legal."

"Well, it ain't right."

"Nope."

"So, what's this cabin about?"

Henry took a long pull on the water, wishing it was the bourbon that it could never be while his father was beside him, not even at age thirty-seven.

His father's voice grew softer. "I figured you wouldn't build it after—"

Henry's gaze fixed on the horizon.

"After Della done took off on you."

"Yeah, well." Henry stood up, brushed off his pants. "I come from mountaineers. Man's got to have a cabin."

The old man stood, too. "Back to them sleepers."

Two hours later, they lowered the second of the floor beams that defined the cabin's width onto one of the sills that defined its length. With a pencil, Henry marked on the sill the sleeper's end and moved it aside. The old man finished sharpening his axe, and with the finesse of a cake decorator, sliced a lap joint out of the sleeper's end. He tapped it into the sill with a mallet, smoothing his chapped fingers over the notch to show Henry that it was flush with the sill. Finally, the old man bored a hole through both sleeper and sill and hammered in a square locust peg. He looked at his son and handed him the axe and the mallet.

Later, after Henry had done well enough with his lap joint and flush sill and locust peg to repair his pride, he smiled as he looked at his cabin, six inches higher than it was the last time they'd worked on it. His shoulders ached, new callouses throbbed on his hands, and his cheeks burned from the scour of wind.

8

All was still as Herschel entered his cabin, save the candle flames that flattened in the breeze off the door. He put the lantern on the table that anchored the room as well as their lives, with its two metal plates laid out for breakfast, the Bible cleaved by its red ribbon for the morning's reading, the parts of a rifle he was cleaning. He leaned over Lucy's cradle beside the dark fireplace to check on her and went back to lower the lantern flame. Ruth sat on their bed, tucking a nightgown into a flour sack.

"How much longer you goin' to have to sleep over there?" Herschel asked. He hooked his thumbs into his galluses and pulled them off his shoulders.

"Until she can feed that baby on her own. What little milk we've got she keeps spillin'."

Herschel dropped his pants to the floor, then the pit-stained homespun shirt, and got in bed. "What about Lucy?"

"Yea, she gets her milk first, a'course. Seems like my teats are of a mind to wean her, though. Miss Annaliese needs to hire somebody, a wet nurse, looks like."

"When do you wean a baby?" Herschel pushed his wife down playfully to block her from leaving.

"Around six months." She pressed her body into his that smelled of every minute of today's chores—Herschel's smell—and she found comfort in it. She wedged her head under his chin.

"How you reckon Miss Annaliese is going to bear this without him?"

Ruth didn't trust her voice, so she just shrugged.

"Mr. John was a good man."

She still didn't say anything.

"Ruth?"

She nodded against his chin, but Mr. John was not a good man, not to her. She lay in Herschel's arms as still as a fawn under a bough, praying that the tired arms around her would fall away soon. She stared at the rugged rafters.

John Stregal started out a good man. Two years earlier when he hired her and Herschel, he treated her with respect, like a daughter, really. He paid good wages and paid on time, never pushed them into unsafe work, gave them every Sunday and Christian holiday off. She loved watching his children climb into his lap for stories and the tender attentions of his big hands. Not a cheating bone in his body, money-wise or floozy-wise. But he changed. He got so that he riled easily, cussed and pissed without a care as to who heard or saw, ran around the grounds willy nilly like some rabid dog. While Annaliese tried to deal with his wild spending, his sleepless nights, and the anger that drove the children away, Ruth just tried to stay out of his way. But over time, she saw a new look in his eyes when they landed on her. He found reasons for her to deliver meals to his office, and she ran out of reasons not to.

Sometimes, the memory of that day in the office still woke her in the middle of the night—the stench of his whiskey as he pinned her hands above her head, the metallic clink of his belt being unbuckled. It happened twice, seeding in her an all-consuming hatred she'd never known even in her grim youth, so it was without a grain of guilt that she fouled the meals she brought him with plants that gave him the scours and sent him outside to retch and heave. He got the message, left her alone after that. She never said a word to anyone. Herschel would've murdered him. Later, when her monthlies stopped and her breasts ached so much she couldn't stand the softest cotton brushing across, she knew the child hadn't sprung from Herschel's seed. He'd planted so many, but her womb, like the arid ground of the Bible where seeds shriveled into death, couldn't nurture life, or so she thought.

One day, Annaliese came to her cabin door and when Ruth opened it, slapped her hard. Pushing Ruth inside, she screamed terrible things about her, said that she saw John jump out at her from behind the chicken coop, saw Ruth's scowl that said there was history there, heard their argument that was beyond that of employer and employee. Ruth cried out the truth, but Annaliese wouldn't hear it.

When Ruth's belly overwhelmed her tiny frame, John's madness was clear to everyone on the property, and Annaliese eventually softened. Ruth told her that a baby was all she'd ever wanted, a gift from God she thought would never be hers to hold. Annaliese told Ruth that in that case, she was happy for her and it didn't matter who the father was.

Over time, though, it did, of course.

Listening to Herschel's snores, Ruth wanted nothing more than to remain cocooned with him for the night, for the month, for eternity. The rafters overhead were pressing the breath out of her. In them, she saw Annaliese's expression from earlier that day in the kitchen as she looked at the two babies in their baskets—one child with perfect lips and fat cheeks, and the other whose face would draw looks of alarm and pity for the rest of her life, unless she got it fixed, if she got that far.

9

Canton, Georgia

At midnight, Olive Washburn was ten-in-the-morning awake as she sat on her bed. She gripped the flour sack she had packed with a shawl, her Bible, some biscuits, and the tattered newspaper article with the photograph that she had looked at too many times. The money was long gone. It was time for her to get what they owed her.

She heard the neighbors returning home from the mill's second shift. Throughout the mill village, their windows went dark one by one. Into the silver moonlight she slipped, tiptoeing past the families who had loaned her money, avoiding the blinding light cast by the vast electrified cotton mill, picking her way to the road out of town. Black forest, where night creatures waited in the earth's seeping warmth to sink fangs and claws into flesh, swallowed the dirt path. She kept to center.

At dawn, she met a buckboard at a fork in the road. While the driver studied her without a word, she pulled her shawl tighter and returned his scrutiny with equal measure. Eventually, he took off his hat and she saw that he had kind eyes, so she spoke, then he. His destination wasn't hers—Pinch, Georgia, two counties away—but he was headed that way. Olive climbed into the back of his wagon to sit against splinters and itchy sacks of grain, and she was glad for it.

On the third day of strangers' kindnesses, she rolled into Pinch in a wagon full of cotton bales, tin buckets, broken leather harnesses, and bridles. The driver steered his horse toward the livery's water trough.

Olive jumped out and started to show the driver her empty pockets, but he waved her off and began unloading. She sat on the bench in front of Chastain's General Store to figure out her next move. People bustled in and out of its weather-beaten screen doors, baskets in hand, dragging handkerchiefs across sweaty necks. In an alley, a rooster charged at a cow, driving it backwards into its own still-warm piles. A swarm of quivering piglets encircled a sow that rooted through a pile of garbage with its moist snout. Two women passed the stranger on the bench and dipped their straw hats at her. Ignoring them, Olive scanned the rest of the establishments. She settled on Meddling's Boarding House.

A wide hall cleaved the boarding house into dining room and parlor, both full of customers, mostly men. The scent of roasted meats and yeast rolls, coffee and tobacco swept over Olive as she opened the door, nearly bringing her to her knees she was so hungry. She pressed on down the hall that was plastered with sun-bleached, green-and-white wallpaper of pastoral scenes. It peeled apart at every seam. She passed the dining room where cutlery clinked against ceramic plates. At the end of the hall, two fiftyish women standing at a counter looked over from their conversation.

"Hey," Olive called out.

"Afternoon," said the fleshier of the two watching her approach. She raised a hand to urge disobedient strands of hay-colored hair into her bun. "Help ye?" Her face was as white and plump as biscuit dough.

"Hey," Olive said again as she arrived at the counter. "I'm Olive."

"Thessalonia Meddling, proprietress," the woman said. She pointed her thumb at her companion. "This here's Corinthia, my sister."

"Hey," Corinthia said. She was an older, pastier version of Thessalonia, with deep fissures gripping the downturned mouth. A schoolmarmish authority came across even in that one word. As she looked Olive over, the expression on her long face was one of judgments gathering and barely restrained. The scent of cinnamon floated out of the dining room, but Corinthia looked as though she smelled cow manure.

"Might be a while before we could serve ye," Thessalonia said softly. "We're powerful busy on Mondays."

"Oh, no, that ain't my aim," Olive said. "Wonderin' if you could tell me where I might could find a Mrs. Stregal. Annaliese Stregal."

Thessalonia's eyes slid over to Corinthia's then back. "What fer?" she asked.

"Just want to talk t'her is all," Olive said with a shrug.

Corinthia came around the counter. Her eyes widened at Olive's considerable bosom, big pillowy breasts that challenged the buttons of her bodice (challenged each other, in fact).

Olive pulled her shawl over her chest. "I ain't lookin' fer no trouble."

"I'm thinkin' trouble finds you," Corinthia said.

"Now, Corinthia," Thessalonia said.

Corinthia leaned against the counter. "Which cotton mill you from?" she asked, pointing at the white lint that peppered Olive's brown hair.

Olive batted at her hair. "If you could jest tell me where to find Mrs. Stregal," she said.

"This ain't a good time," Corinthia said. "She had a baby five days ago."

"Oh, really?" Olive asked, suddenly smiling broadly. "No foolin'?"

"What are you grinnin' about?" Thessalonia asked.

"I need work. Anybody with a new baby needs help," Olive said.

"She's got help," Corinthia said.

"Not like the kind of help I can give," Olive said as she turned away. She hurried to the front door, swerving around a group of men on their way out of the dining room who checked her backside.

"Somethin's dead up the creek there if you ask me," Corinthia said.

Thessalonia took a straw hat off the coat rack and handed it to her sister. "Won't take her long to find her. Better get on over there 'fore she does."

10

After a few questions around town, the town in which information about Annaliese Stregal was valuable currency eagerly spent, Olive had the address. She walked the street of modest houses and knocked on the front door of the house she'd expected to be grander. It was only two stories, unpainted like the others, with a skinny porch along the front and sides. Two plain windows to the left of the front door and two to the right, nothing special in her view. The porch floor was furry with ferns sprouting from matching blue pots along the rail posts. She'd seen them in the Sears, Roebuck & Company catalog, the pots, along with a lot of other things she aimed to have one day, such as the green brocade draperies at Mrs. Stregal's windows.

A young woman opened the door, fleshy baby on her bony hip.

"Afternoon," Olive said.

"Afternoon," Ruth said with a long look at the dust-covered woman. "Corinthia said you was comin'."

"Lookin' for Mrs. Stregal," Olive said. "This her place?"

Ruth nodded again.

"Heard she might could use some help."

"Don't 'spect so," Ruth said slowly. "Me and my husband, we take care of things."

"Not that kinda help," Olive said. "I heard at the mercantile that she's got a harelip baby I might could help you with. Heard it, you know, in the back where the women get together behind them bolts of cloth. Harelip babies, they can be hard to feed."

Ruth shifted the baby to her other hip and brushed a fly off her head.

"Shore am sorry to hear about that baby. Mrs. Stregal must be plumb wore out and worried t'death." Olive nodded toward the ragged new-baby cry in the house.

Ruth started closing the door.

"I wonder if I might could trouble you for a drink of water? I've done come all the way from Canton."

Ruth led her around back to the porch, showed her to a rocking chair, and went inside. Olive ran her hand over the quilt that hung over the back of the chair, lingered on what she recognized as a broderie perse vase against a carefully matched background of yellow cotton, and thought that perhaps the inside of the house had more to offer than she thought.

Ruth returned with a pitcher of water and plate of gingerbread squares. "You come all the way from Canton jest for work?" she asked.

"Cherokee's a dirt poor county. Hard to get work there." Olive shoved the gingerbread into her mouth.

"This one here's the poorest county in Georgia."

"Cain't blame a body for tryin'," Olive said, spewing crumbs.

"But you had work." Ruth pointed at her hair. "Cotton mill, looks like."

Olive clawed at her hair. "Cain't live on them wages."

"No husband?" Ruth asked.

Olive opened her mouth to speak, but the new-baby cry was getting closer. Annaliese opened the screened door with the frantic baby crying into her shoulder. "Ruth, can you try to give us some milk?" she asked.

Olive rose from the rocking chair.

Annaliese took a step back, clutched the baby closer.

"Oh, she was jest leavin'," Ruth said. She made collecting motions at Olive and her gingerbread crumbs.

Olive came toward Annaliese with a toothy grin. "Pleased to meet you, Mrs. Stregal. I'm Olive." She took her time looking over the woman she'd wondered about for more than three years. There was the lovely face she'd envisioned, though the deep crow's-feet were a surprise, as were the gray swags under her eyes. Wispy blonde hair fanned across her shoulders and down her nightgown sleeves. The widow's slender frame, bent under the weight of too much death and this yowling infant, held but a whisper of the dignified bearing Olive expected of a prosperous lumberman's wife.

Annaliese barely glanced at Olive. She tried to pull Ruth into the house. "Ruth," she said. "Please."

Despite Annaliese's maneuvering, Olive got a good look at the infant's mouth. "Here. Give her here," she said, reaching for the baby. "I already heard about the baby's mouth."

Annaliese took another step back as Ruth moved in between the two.

"I got what you need, ma'am," Olive said. "Look here." She sat down and unbuttoned her dress, unleashing swollen breasts. "Give her here. I seen this kinda mouth before and I know how to get milk in her." Droplets of milk were already oozing from Olive's brown nipples.

Annaliese looked at the bosoms that clearly were offering more than any other bosoms on the porch and took a step forward. "She can't suck," she said.

"Yes, ma'am, I know." Olive tugged on Annaliese's sleeve, and she finally handed over the infant.

"Ain't you jest the prettiest little thing," Olive said to the baby.

Annaliese and Ruth looked at each other.

Olive braced the child's back and head with her arm and aimed her nipple at her mouth. The baby jerked side to side, arched her back, but Olive calmly insisted until she had shot so much in that the baby had to swallow. Once that was down, Olive aimed the next dose, and soon an easy rhythm was going. Georgia Ann's smacking noises filled the air. The two were drenched. Olive held on tight to nipple and child.

"Would you look at that," Ruth said.

"Shhhh!" Annaliese said, wiping her nose with her sleeve.

"What's her name?" Olive whispered.

"Georgia Ann," Annaliese said.

Annaliese and Ruth leaned against the porch rail, transfixed on nature's simple, timeless ritual and bitterly aware that sometimes the ritual wasn't so simple. In the distance, the mournful whistle of the four-fifteen from Chattanooga floated through the trees. The living room clock chimed four times, paused, then finished with its quick chime chime for the quarter hour. Beyond the porch, the world flowed on its usual currents, unimpressed by the dumb luck that had just walked up Annaliese Stregal's front path.

11

Annaliese bolted upright from a nap so heavy she didn't recognize her own walls for a minute. As the fog cleared, she saw that there was her bureau, her window framed in white lawn. Crib. Georgia Ann's crib. Too quiet.

She eased her legs over the side of the bed and crept over. The baby slept on her back in baby bliss. A thin ribbon of drool shone on her cheek. Annaliese put her fingers lightly on the tiny chest to confirm its rise and fall. The hall clock chimed six times, which meant Georgia Ann had been asleep for almost two hours. Annaliese stared at the full belly, swollen and beautiful.

The doorknob rattled softly and let Ruth and Lucy in. "Praise be," Ruth said over the newborn. "Two whole hours."

The women stared at the baby and the mouth that still shocked them. Annaliese looked over at Lucy's mouth.

Ruth pulled her daughter closer. "I'm sorry what's happened to this new baby. I hate that this has happened to you, to us. We're family, Miss Annaliese. Remember?"

Annaliese struggled to fight back tears.

Georgia Ann's eyes fluttered open, then closed again.

Ruth pulled Annaliese toward the bureau. "Let's get you a bath, some fresh clothes," she whispered, opening a drawer. "The kettles are on downstairs. That woman is watchin' 'em. You'll feel so much better."

In the hall, Annaliese put her hands out and stopped. "Wait. Where are we going to put her? She's got to be here to feed the baby in the night."

"You want to turn her loose in the house? We don't know the first thing 'bout her, her people."

"If we put a cot for her here—" Annaliese's hands laid out a cot along the wall.

"Don't even know her last name."

"We could put another cot for you here." She pointed to the second envisioned cot. "To keep an eye on her."

"Oh."

"Herschel will understand."

Ruth ran her hands up and down her apron over that assumption. "She's prob'ly got lice."

"Ruth."

The girl headed for her kitchen, where she was certain that trouble— tucked into salvation's pocket—now sat at her table.

Annaliese followed her into the kitchen's aromas of browning loaves and fresh coffee. At the table, Olive peeled a potato over a blue and white enamel bowl. Annaliese opened a cabinet and stood there for a moment trying to remember what she'd gone there to get. Pink rosebud cups were piled in a stack next to saucers. Plates were on the shelf above. Cups. That was it. Coffee.

Ruth pulled the loaves out of the oven.

Annaliese poured some coffee and sat down near Olive to savor the quiet house, the immaculate white wall tiles bathed in the late afternoon light, and this one blessed moment when her body didn't leak anything. Looking over the rim of the cup, she judged Olive to be about thirty years old, although she had learned that the lines etched in an Appalachian woman's face had more to do with dawn-to-dusk chores and poor diet than the passage of years, so Olive could've been in her early twenties. Her cheeks were clear, no dark patches from pellagra, so her health was likely good enough. The brown hair was dull and flecked with white specks of lint. No lice that she could see. A luscious pair of plump lips were out of proportion to her small face, as were those bosoms to her frame. Olive looked back at Annaliese with saucy brown eyes.

"So grateful that you came along," Annaliese said.

Olive smiled and focused on the potato in her hand. "Glad I can help, ma'am," she said.

"So you've seen other babies like mine?"

Olive nodded. "The babies of kin, neighbors."

"How many live past infancy?"

Ruth moved the kettles off the stove. "Your bath?"

"Yes, yes, in a minute," Annaliese said, raising the steaming cup of coffee at her to show that it was still full.

"Once they get to where they can eat table food, they come out all right," Olive said.

Annaliese leaned forward. "Later, are they able to talk plain? Are they understood?"

Ruth came over to the table. "You know, I been tryin' to feed her. Squeezin' and mashin' these teats of mine jest to get a few drops into a cup."

Annaliese took a sip of coffee to hide her irritation.

Olive shook her head at Ruth. "You can't get all tense about it. It takes relaxin' to get the milk goin'."

"I ain't tense," Ruth said. "It jest takes bosoms like yorn."

"What about her being able to talk clearly?" Annaliese asked again. "Will people understand her?"

"Depends on how bad that hole inside of her mouth is." Olive put the peeled potato in the bowl and plucked another from a bag at her feet.

Annaliese stared at the table for a while. "Where are you from?"

"Canton."

"How'd you get here?" Ruth asked.

"Couple of wagon rides."

Annaliese nodded. "Good-sized town, Canton. My husband had occasional business there, cruising timber land for lease, he said, before the children and I arrived two years ago."

Olive studied the shiny contours of the potato. "Sorry for your loss, ma'am. Mine's done passed too."

"I'm sorry," Annaliese said.

"How'd you know that Mr. Stregal passed?" Ruth asked, leaning down and turning her head sideways to make Olive look at her.

Olive reached under the table for her flour sack and pulled out a newspaper page. "Seen it here," she said.

Annaliese reached for the crumbling page. The obituary photo of John, nearly the size of a deck of cards, gave her a jolt.

"Why are you carryin' this around?" Ruth asked. "He's been gone for five months."

Annaliese looked up from the newspaper.

"There's a little about Mrs. Stregal at the end there," Olive said, pointing. "Says you're a community leader. I thought, a kind lady like you, maybe you'd let me work for you."

"You went and got somebody to read this to you?" Ruth asked.

Olive gave her a measured look. "I didn't go get nobody. One of the spinners was reading it to some of us 'cause we recognized Mr. Stregal there from the day the mill owner brung him through the spinnin' room, showed him around. He came over to us to say hey."

"But why'd you wait till now?" Ruth asked.

"I had a baby. She took sick and I had to stop work. When she died a couple months back, I tried to make money feeding babies."

"Oh, my," Annaliese said. "I'm so sorry." She patted Olive's hand and looked over at Ruth whose face finally softened a little.

"I went back to my shift at the mill, nursed babies at night, but I just couldn't keep it up. The dust got in my lungs so bad, it was leave that place or die."

Annaliese folded the newspaper quietly. "I can see why you left. So this article brought you to me?"

"Yes. I didn't know you'd had a baby, ma'am."

"All right," Annaliese said.

"In the Canton mill, it's eleven hours a day, six days a week. Thirty cents a day, not that I ever held a dollar of mill wages. You get paid with checks, and only place you can use 'em is the company store. Here, I hope I can make good money, especially with you, Mrs. Stregal."

Another question was brewing on Ruth's restless face. Annaliese gave her a look that made her cross her arms even tighter. "I hear that children work in those cotton mills," Annaliese said.

"Yes, ma'am, they're workin' under them hissin' machines, sweepin' up scraps of cotton off them wet floors eleven hours a day."

"Wet floors? That don't make no sense a'tall," Ruth said.

"The company pumps steam in, keeps the windows closed to keep the fibers soft for processin', they say." Olive spat the words out. "So there's the dust and the awful racket. If you're tall enough on tiptoe to reach a spinnin' frame, you can work. Mill owners work 'em young as five."

"What do they have a five-year-old do?" Annaliese asked.

"Any kinda cleanin' or machine repair in a small, tight space."

"Last winter, a boy got his arm caught in a shaftin' wheel that spun him around pert near a hunnert times afore they could stop the machine. They was goin' to amputate but he died first, a'course. Ten years old. Hit like to kill his Mama but next day she brought his little brother to work in the weavin' room. All that racket, he'll be deaf 'fore long. Children ain't on the mill books, but they're workin'. Yes, ma'am."

"What's your last name?" Annaliese asked.

"Washburn. Mrs. Olive Washburn."

"Well, you've found a job here, Mrs. Washburn," Annaliese said.

"That sounds mighty nice, Mrs. Stregal," Olive said. She let her second potato, finally skinned and glistening like a wet snake, slide into the bowl.

12

Seven days after Georgia Ann's birth, Annaliese felt fossilized still, tethered to crib and bed. Even when she thought she might have the strength to walk into town, she sent Herschel for the mail so she wouldn't have to face questions about the baby. Sooner or later, she knew, there would be one question too many and she'd be in tears. When women brought covered dishes to the door, Ruth accepted, thanked, and dismissed as quickly as possible. Wherever Georgia Ann was when the knock came, Annaliese made sure she took her out of sight. Henry kept a respectable distance, merely writing notes to offer help. She sent word back that everything was fine. Every day that passed with Georgia Ann filling her stomach with milk moved that lie closer to the truth.

One morning, Ruth opened the door to find someone without food. Wade McClain pulled off his hat and grinned at her as he smoothed his long, coal-black hair.

"Wade," Ruth said. "What's wrong? Somethin' wrong up at the mill, ain't it?"

"Nice to see you, too, Ruth."

"Well, come in, a'course, but you know what I mean. Why else would you be here?" She opened the door wider and waved him in. "Wipe your feet there."

Annaliese appeared at the top of the stairs. Webs of fire went up her neck at the sight of the sawmill's supervisor. She ran toward him. "Wade! What's wrong?"

Wade ran a hand down his legs. "I hate to barge in here when you're tryin' to rest and all."

"Wade, I know you didn't ride two hours from the sawmill without good reason," Annaliese said.

"No, ma'am."

Ruth put her hands on her hips and nodded.

"Let's go in here," Annaliese said, gesturing at the parlor. They settled into chairs. Ruth pulled the pocket doors closed.

"You've got to come back to live at the sawmill," he said.

"Oh my goodness, Wade. I can't—"

"Them hills is crawling with fellers from off and they ain't worryin' about property lines with their cruisin' and cuttin'."

"Are you saying they're cutting timber on my land?"

"To get the poplars, yes, ma'am, because some garment factory in the north has put out a big call for long and wide lumber for sewing tables, and—"

"Who's doing this?"

"Don't rightly know, there's so many."

"Did you fetch the sheriff?"

"He ain't gonna pay a Cherokee no mind, Miss Annaliese, but you—"

"Those men think I won't do anything."

"Maybe."

"Because I'm a woman."

"Maybe they reckon you just ain't payin' attention."

Annaliese shifted in her chair.

"Ma'am, with one whole slope of Black Face Mountain bein' nothin' but your seedlings that you planted, them loggers might start drivin' the wagons across it to get to wherever they're aimin' to go."

"Across my seedlings? Oxen and wagons tearing through my seedlings?"

"Might."

Annaliese shook her head. "I have a one-week-old baby. And my sister will be bringing Sam and Emmie back soon."

"You got a right nice house for everybody to live in up there."

"But I'm not ready to call the timber crews back or even decide what to do with the company at all."

"Ma'am, I think you want them thievin' loggers to see your timber crews out in them woods."

"What about sending out the skeleton crew that's taking care of the mill?"

"Jest eight of 'em ma'am, and they're the first to tell you they don't cut timber."

"So start the company back up?" She leaned back. "I'd need to know what to cut, what to leave, what to plant, and where."

"Miss Annaliese, you do know." He pressed his palms toward her. "When you gave me some of your land last year, you and I read them government circulars and journals about forestry." He looked at the table beside his chair and picked up *Forest Quarterly Magazine*. "I know you been readin' this."

She nodded.

"'Course you have. So, you do know."

"But run the business? There's the market to follow, the equipment and buildings to take care of, the hiring and firing. There's always some shiftless soul on the crew dodging the law."

"Ma'am, I—"

"Timbering is changing so fast, Wade."

"Sure is. Them loggers is movin' faster than fire."

Annaliese looked out the window.

Wade wiped his forehead with the inside of his elbow. "Well, then, you reckon you might could get somebody else to hold down the sawmill till you're ready? Somebody white?"

Annaliese turned back to him. "What happened?"

"Nothin', nothin'." He looked at the floor.

"Wade."

"They shot my coon hound. Dumped him in a well."

"You think it was our own workers? One of our eight?"

"It ain't gone over well that a Cherokee is sittin' in Mr. John's office."

"You'd think they'd be grateful I've kept them on the payroll."

"For doin' pretty much nothin', yes ma'am."

"Can't you hang on a little longer?"

Wade wiped his hand over his face. "How about selling the place?"

"And let someone brutalize my land?" She watched him worry the rim of his hat. He knew what he was asking of her. The lumber business was unregulated and risky, driven by the unforgiving forces of nature and market, and fueled by male hubris. It could flatten her and her yellow sunbonnet within months. She'd heard the joke at her own dinner table when John and his brother talked business: The way to make a small fortune in the lumber business is to start with a large one.

But there was change coming to the owning and managing of forested land, or so the journals said. *Practical forestry*, it was called. She might not have the energy, but she darn well had enough money and outrage to try it.

"Let me think about this," she said and she showed him the door.

13

Henry smoothed his crisp white shirt, wiggled the knot of his tie, and knocked on the front door.

Annaliese opened it almost immediately, wide-brim straw hat in hand. Even through the screened door he could see that her eyes shimmered with energy, her cheeks glowed with health. Her smile emboldened him to pull the screened door at the same time she was pushing it open, so they almost collided. Inches from her eyes, he searched them for a trace of excitement. He thought he saw a flare of it from those blue depths. Taking her hand, he whispered, "Anna, I've been so worried."

She squeezed his fingers. Deep inside the house, the baby was crying.

"How's she doing?"

"She's up to seven pounds, thank God."

From the street, two women slowed their stroll to watch them.

Annaliese pulled her hand away. "We should go," she said as she swept her hat onto her topknot. She raised her voice to say, "So kind of you to pick up my family at the depot, Mr. Chastain."

At the buggy, she accepted his hand and climbed onto the seat where he had laid a clean blanket. With a soft snap of the reins, Henry got the horse going for what he had just signaled was to be the slowest haul of her life, a pace more bovine than equine. She lifted and plopped her woody hooves along the road of houses snuggled into their flowerbeds. Henry was grateful to see unattended windows and empty rockers on the porches.

Annaliese closed her eyes to take in the scent that had just found her. "Oh, the lilacs," she said.

"Your first time outside in sixteen days."

She waved a hand at the two gawkers. "You've been counting, Mr. Chastain?" she asked.

"Annaliese, I've been watching for you to appear at my door. I shouldn't tell you that, I guess." Henry put the reins in one hand and placed the other close to hers on the seat. The horse continued her glacial pace. Ahead, in the front yard of a brick one-story with a welcoming apron of wide steps, children pulled on a goat harnessed to cart. A dog nipped at its hooves. The goat stood firmly entrenched in resistance.

She slid her hand across the bench seat to take his. "Henry, I'm sorry that I didn't come," she said. "I didn't want to be around people, didn't want to smile and answer questions about the baby. The truth is, I'm dreading walking into the train station in a few minutes."

The horse started a turn onto the main road into town. Henry wanted to pull her back to the longer route where the homes thinned out, but a train whistle floated over the treetops.

She started wagging her foot. "I talked to Wade yesterday," she said.

"Wade? He was here in town?"

"He says people are cutting my timber."

"He should've come to me about that."

"He says I need to come back. Says I need to send my crews back out there."

Henry raised his eyebrows. "For you to send crews. You, literally."

"Yes."

"Wish he'd talked to me first." Henry ran his hand along his leg. "It shouldn't be you."

She looked at him.

"Not now, I mean."

"But he's right. I can't continue to neglect the land. Land always needs minding."

"It's a lot of land, Anna."

"John left the company in good shape," she said. "You and I have been over the books," she said.

"Ah, you're wanting to sell it. Thank heavens. I thought you meant—"

"And let someone clear cut my land?"

Henry shook his head. "As your legal counsel and friend and person with good sense, I advise you to wait on this decision."

"But while I wait, greed is ruining our mountains."

Henry rubbed his fingers over the reins.

"I can't wait, Henry. Think of the beauty that once was. Miles and miles of the primeval forest before Europeans arrived. The animals, the waters, the wildflowers. We've lost so much of that beauty that took millions of years to evolve. Unique, ancient trees, now gone forever. I have to save what's left. Even the moss at our feet deserves to be saved."

"It's a hardwood timber company, Annaliese."

"I have an idea."

"Oh Lord."

"Before Georgia Ann was born, I read about this forester that George Vanderbilt brought over from Germany four years ago to manage the forests on his North Carolina estate. More than a hundred-twenty-thousand acres."

"In Asheville, uh huh."

"No one else in North America is trying to rehabilitate American forests. This German says we can nurture them as well as profit from them."

"The government's working on this, you know."

"The Forest Reserve Act? That's just setting aside forests, not managing what's privately held."

Henry leaned closer to take her hand. "Anna, I can hire crews for you and get Hoyt to come back and supervise them. Until you get your strength back."

"But Hoyt doesn't know anything about these scientific principles from Europe. I want to try them. If not me, then who else?"

"George Vanderbilt?"

"Henry, I have the money and the time to steward the land the way this German man describes."

"The time? You've got a two-week-old baby."

Annaliese stared at the floorboards, resisting the burden of Henry's realistic reasoning. Within the hour, her house would be chaos, the baby hungry and crying, Sam and Emmie recoiling from the sight of their little sister, Ruth trying to soothe, and Henry watching it all, being right. She wagged her foot faster. Her priority needed to be the baby, one pound at a time, and her other children still reeling from so much.

14

Henry and Annaliese rushed onto the platform in time to see the locomotive grinding to a halt, belching steam and grit into the faces of the few waiting there. A woman started toward Annaliese with her hand held out, as if to offer a word. Henry saw her coming and handed his handkerchief to Annaliese, which she used to dab at supposed grit in her eyes long enough for the woman to hesitate, then turn away.

First off was the conductor, barking unintelligible announcements. On his heels came eight-year-old Samuel, then Emeline, two years younger, to charge through the steam toward their mother with such glee that Henry put his hand at her back to brace her. He thought it best merely to pat their heads, but Emeline raised her arms to him. With her sticky face pressed against his, he watched for the rest of the family, and soon Annaliese's sister appeared in the doorway, struggling with a large valise and an enormous hat alive with fluttering feathers. He put Emeline down.

"Welcome back, Mrs. Van," he said, taking the valise from her with one hand and offering her the other.

Dorothy Van came down the steps and accepted it. She was a taller, more angular version of Annaliese, but she had the same heart-shaped face and delicate mouth. "Mr. Chastain, oh, thank goodness for you," she said.

Her husband, Phillip, followed her down the steps with a package in his arms. The two men nodded at each other.

Annaliese rushed over to kiss and hug her sister while the children clung to her like cockleburs. At this embrace, the first long, warm physical contact she'd had for months and with this woman whose life pages held so many of the same pressed flowers as did hers, Annaliese began to cry. The sisters held onto each other for a long time. Finally, they stepped apart.

"Mother sends her love," Dorothy said, batting away tears. "She'll come as soon as she can walk. That darn foot that won't heal."

"I know," Annaliese said.

"But she sent this," Phillip said, holding his package higher.

"It's a kitchen scale, Mama," Samuel shouted. "For weighing the baby."

Annaliese burst into tears again.

The train whistle startled all of them away from the tracks. Phillip and Henry gently herded everyone through the depot doors and into the moment Annaliese was dreading.

When they pulled up to Annaliese's house, Ruth and Olive rose from the porch rockers. Dorothy rushed up the steps, took Olive's hands to pump them up and down, and stole a glance at the chest she'd heard so much about. Ruth wrapped her arms around the children and guided them to the basket beside a rocker. Georgia Ann peered up at them from a froth of bonnet ruffles. Emeline leaned back slightly, clamped her hand over her mouth.

Samuel alternated between looking at the baby and up at his mother. "What happened to her, Mama?" he asked.

Annaliese couldn't speak.

"Sam, we talked about this," Dorothy said as she patted the boy's back.

Samuel reached for one of the baby's fingers. He swung it gently back and forth. Behind him, Emeline frowned.

Ruth sidled over to Annaliese. "They'll be alright, Miss Anna," she whispered.

For a long while, no one in the circle moved, save Henry, who placed his hand again at the small of Annaliese's back for bracing.

Emeline Stregal would not come one inch closer. With locked knees, she stood at the threshold of her mother's bedroom, arms crossed as she watched her mother and brother put the baby in her crib.

"Why does she look like that, Mama?" Samuel asked, peering down at the face.

"Sometimes this happens."

"But how?" The boy put his hand on his mother's arm.

"I don't know. Only God knows, Sam." She pulled him into a hug.

"Will she always look like that?"

"Maybe not. When she's bigger, maybe a surgeon can do something about it." Out of the corner of her eye, Annaliese saw Emeline backing away.

"Would you stay here with the baby while she sleeps?"

Annaliese took Emeline's hand and led her to her bedroom where they snuggled into each other on the bed.

"She scares me," Emeline said.

"I know, Emmie."

"I don't want to look at her again."

Annaliese tried to make slow, calm circles on her back while her own heartbeat pounded in her ears.

Emeline burrowed into her mother's side. They lay silent for a while, listening to the murmur of conversation downstairs, the wagons rattling by, the staccato barking of the Millers' dog next door. Thunder echoed in the valley, and they waited for Mrs. Miller to call the children in. Downstairs, Olive's strident voice pierced the civilized hum of the other adults' conversation.

"Who's that woman?" Emeline asked.

"She's going to be here for a while, honey. She's feeding Georgia."

"Is she going to sleep in here?"

"No. She sleeps in one of those cots out in the hall."

"For how long?"

"As long as the baby needs milk."

The rain arrived in a soft drumming on the roof, prompting Annaliese to grope for the quilt at their feet.

"I'm glad we're home," Emeline said. Annaliese pulled the quilt over them. "I don't ever want to leave here again, Mama." Emeline threw an arm over her mother's chest. The raindrops came faster, a thousand soft brushes sweeping pollen to the rivulets and minerals to busy roots. Emeline's breathing fell into a steady rhythm. A few weeks ago, that rhythm, the warmth of her precious daughter, the rain—all of it would've lulled Annaliese to sleep too, but not today.

When the drumming had moved on, she heard voices at the front door— loud, excited voices, not family. She slipped out from under Emeline and closed the door softly. Samuel and the baby were not in her room.

Corinthia and Thessalonia Meddling stood in the doorway, covered dishes in hand, cooing at the baby that Dorothy was displaying like a blue- ribbon pumpkin.

"Isn't she just precious?" Dorothy was saying when Annaliese swept in with her heart in her throat at the sight of the first townsfolk who'd made it past her doorjamb since the birth. Annaliese guessed that the Meddlings had heard that Dorothy and Phillip were in town and, betting on one of them opening the door, had swept up some of the boarding house's fried chicken and whatever and hurried over.

Dorothy turned around at the sound of her sister's steps. Georgia Ann's fingers were curled over the edge of her blanket as though she knew to hold on while being swung through the air by new arms. Her eyes were wide open, flitting around. Dorothy said, "Anna, look who's come to meet Georgie," and before Annaliese could snatch her baby from her sister's arms, Dorothy swung back to the Meddlings.

Corinthia leaned in, carefully controlling her face. The rheumy eyes flared. Muscles twitched. Thessalonia joined her in breathless staring. They clutched their fried chicken to their bosoms.

Annaliese closed the door a few inches toward them, but they took no notice.

Thessalonia squeezed Annaliese's arm. "Darlin', she has such pretty hands," she said.

Dorothy winced at this well-known dodge that women used when they couldn't find anything complimentary to say.

"So nice of you to drop by," Annaliese said, closing the door a little more. She didn't reach to take the food, already rancid in her mouth.

Dorothy handed her the baby and took the dishes, and soon Corinthia and Thessalonia were stepping around puddles in the yard.

15

Rabun County, Georgia

Dawson pulled his horse to a halt at the crest of a ridge to look over what he guessed to be about another day's ride—thirty miles between him and the Tallulah Falls gorge in Rabun County, where the Tallulah River raced down a canyon said to be one thousand feet deep. The locals said that you could hear the roar of the falls for miles. To his right, a rocky ledge jutted chest-high into his view. He grabbed hold of a bush growing out of it and leaned out to study the contours of the valley. To his left and ahead, he saw rolling hills that he could easily cross. He fished his binoculars out of his left pocket.

For a few miles on both sides of a chiseled rock face, the land was denuded except for the usual carnage left behind by loggers. Dawson tilted the binoculars to follow a river uphill. A team of oxen were pulling up to it with a load of enormous logs. Another crew beating him to some timber.

He picked up the reins too hard, which startled the horse into backing up into the granite ledge that was the beginning of a shallow cave. A rattle from deep within its darkness made Dawson's heart stop. Slowly he turned and saw four yellow reptilian pupils, four pinhole nostrils. A second wave of rattles started up. Dawson eased off the horse and tied her to a tree. He found a limb he judged to be stout enough and long enough and jumped onto the ledge above the den. With a few underhand jabs, he provoked the two snakes into the sun. He leveled his Colt .45 and within six shots had slowed them enough that he could take his time reloading the cylinder and emptying it again into their twitching bodies.

Dawson got the horse settled down and headed for Tallulah Falls thinking of a hot bath, Early Times whiskey, laundered clothes, a tender steak, and the letter he expected to be waiting for him at the post office. He kicked the horse into a trot. Spring tourists, drawn to the falls by ads and flyers, would fill all of the hotels by dusk.

The post office clerk was turning the sign on his door to Closed when Dawson shoved his way in. The letter, addressed to Elijah Dawson, was withdrawn from a dusty shelf and handed over with a scowl. Even as buggies began stacking up at the hotel entrance across the street, Dawson stopped to rip into the envelope.

Chaug Kia Kin, China
February 4, 1903

My dear brother:
Your letter reached me last Sunday. I thank you heartily for the news of your labors in the Georgia mountains and your good health. I want to assure you that God has granted me good health as well, a blessing indeed when so many of my missionary brethren have fallen to malignant smallpox, sepsis, leprosy, and typhoons. In my good constitution and in my fruitful work here in Chaug Kia Kin, I believe that your prayers and mine have been answered.

The clamor for Bibles in China is greater than ever. The leaven of Divine Truth that has been stirred into this bowl of error and corruption is rising! The natives desire the sacred pages that they may understand the way of eternal life, though I will admit conversions are slow. We can only pray that as they receive and study the Truth, God will bless this Truth to the salvation of their souls. People far away in the interior of this country who have never seen a missionary send requests for copies of what they call "The Heavenly Treasure." By my reckoning, we need to print 1,500 more Bibles for them and for my growing congregation here as soon as possible.

Meanwhile, in Tung-Chow, the Rev. A. C. Smith and Rev. R. L. Whilden of the Southern Convention are reporting forty baptisms, eighty Sunday School scholars, a new school, the raising of timbers for a church, and even a native ordained pastor.

But even more successful is a trio of lady missionaries working in the interior. In five years, the ladies are said to have made nearly 1,200 visits to villages, preaching the gospel and establishing schools. They are supported by the Ladies' Missionary Society of the First Baptist Church of Richmond, Virginia. Recently, it was reported that the lady missionaries received $5,000 from their Virginia benefactors to pay for translations in Chinese of hymnals, the Parables of our Lord, and, of course, Bibles. The glorious triumphs of these intrepid travelers are all the more remarkable given their gender.

In truth, I am disheartened by the failure of our Convention to sufficiently support my work, and I will admit to jealousy over those Virginia benefactors. It is my earnest hope to have 1,500 Bibles in hand within three months, and the funds for a church, organ, and furnishings within six. In the past, your support has made possible my dwelling and translations of the Bible into local dialects. I pray that your generosity will endure. I ask for $8,000 to cover the cost of the Bibles ($1,000) and the church ($7,000). If you can provide this as soon possible, I will be able to remain here in this fertile ground to equal, if not surpass, the ladies' accomplishments.

I rejoice that the Lord has counted me worthy to be his ambassador to this vast empire and that He has given me a loyal and generous brother in you, dear Buck. Father and mother would be so proud of your support of what I do.

Fraternally and eternally yours,
Isaiah

Dawson tucked the letter into a pocket. He was not an educated man. He made his way in the world on his wits, a pliable moral compass that condoned the selective application of the Bible's teachings, and luck, such as winning the card game years ago that gave him a lumber company. This kind of money that his brother was asking for broke new ground, though. How could he get that without risking jail? he wondered. He looked across the street. The bags coming off the carriages in front of the hotel likely held jewelry, cash even. But he was too old now to scale walls and climb in windows, too bald and fat to charm the maids into letting him into a hotel room. The easier gold for the stealing was timber that stood out in the open with no one around for miles.

Dawson headed for the hotel, where he would marinate in a tub for a while and ponder his next move.

Around midnight, Dawson laid his third winning hand of sweaty cards on the poker table. Three men leaned back from the table and stole glances at the serial loser—the kid who had a giveaway face that shouldn't be at a poker table—to see if he was fool enough to play another round. The winner was an unsettling sort who had talked nonstop about the Colt .45 justice he delivered in running his timber business.

Dawson picked at a scab on his head. "You're up to $250," he said.

"You need to quit, son," one of the men said to the loser.

"You'll get the money, mister," the kid said. "Deal again. I'll show ya."

Dawson pulled his gun out of his pocket and wobbled to his feet. "I got a better idea." He waved the gun toward the door to the alley.

The three players threw their hands up. "Whoa, mister, hold on," one of them said.

Giveaway Face pushed his chair away from the table slowly and pointed at the other players. "Witnesses here, mister. Three of 'em. If you shoot me, you'll swing for it."

"I see 'em. Let's go." Dawson picked up a lantern, opened the back door, and waited for the young man.

In the alley, Dawson yanked open his collar and brought the lantern closer to a red scar at the top of his chest. "This here's what got done to me after the last poker game I lost." He shoved the kid against a building and put the gun to his chest. "Let me tell you, that bullet went clear through. Tore me up for months. Taught me a lesson, though. I come up with the money." He pointed the revolver at the kid's collarbone.

"Mister, I got a young 'un," the kid said.

"I got a brother in China."

"Huh?"

Dawson cocked the trigger.

"Wait, wait! I know somethin'. Worth more than what I owe you."

Dawson raised an eyebrow.

"The house where I work? Rufus Moss's house. You know who he is?"

"No."

"He built this town. Owns thousands of acres around the Tallulah River and ten of the hotels. Built the big one at the edge of the gorge, you know?"

"You talk too much." Dawson kicked his leg.

"He's powerful important. Last week, I was stackin' wood in a fireplace in his dining room when I heard him talkin' to his brother in the next room. They was talkin' about some man that died in Gilmer County."

Dawson shoved the gun deeper. "So?"

"They said that man owned a couple hunnert acres of big ol' poplars and right now poplars are getting top dollar."

Dawson uncoiled from his crouch.

"The Moss brothers was sayin' they might buy that land." The kid smeared sweat from his eyes with the back of his hand.

"How long ago did you hear this?"

"Last week. Maybe five days ago? So this is worth somethin' to you, right? You said you was in the timber business. So, we're square?"

"Not hardly."

"Swear to God this is true."

"It better be. I know where to find you."

"Swear to God, mister."

Dawson tucked the gun into his pants. "Ye who blasphemes the name of the Lord shall be struck down. Leviticus. Got a good mind to do it to you myself."

"So we're square?" the kid called as Dawson walked away, leaving him unscathed. "Like I said, I've got a young 'un."

The Gilmer County courthouse, a two-story brick building with a clock tower, dominated Pinch's town square, as intended. Dawson walked up its path that led to all the rules and regulations the citizens of the county cared to have and some they didn't. In the foyer, sun streamed in from the tower windows, illuminating every crack in the floor's black-and-white tiles. Dust motes swirled in the current that trailed behind him. He walked past three doors and opened the last one labeled County Tax Assessor.

A raw-boned man with thick spectacles looked up from his filing. "Afternoon," he said, eyeing the visitor's jacket that looked as though it had been picked at by a gang of crows and the pocket that bulged with what was likely a pistol. The jaw and cheeks hadn't seen a razor in a week, maybe two.

"Like to take a look at the tax maps," Dawson said.

The clerk closed the filing cabinet. "You in the lumber business too?"

"Too?"

"Last coupla weeks, I must've had half a dozen fellas from somewhere else wantin' to see who owns what around here." The clerk lifted a large book off a shelf, put it on a table, and waved Dawson over.

"Hell," Dawson said. "Anybody asking about land owned by somebody who died couple months back?"

"That would be the Stregal brothers' land."

"Brothers? They both died?"

"Yes, sir. Terrible thing the way they went."

The clerk leaned toward Dawson to invite questions about the terrible part, but Dawson gave him a flat look. "Well, anyway, nobody's been asking about that land," he said, straightening. "Everybody in north Georgia is giving Mrs. Stregal some respect, some time, before jumpin' on her."

"Mrs. Stregal? Which one?"

"The only one left. John Stregal's widow. Where you from?"

"Tennessee."

"Well, here are the tax maps. For each parcel of property, there's—"

"A number. I know." Dawson sat down and ran his fingers over the yellowed pages.

The clerk brought over paper and a pencil. "After this, you'll be wanting the book of deeds." He tilted his head toward the door. "Across the hall there."

Dawson nodded and began making notes. After a while, he looked up, his finger resting on the map. "She's got parcels all over the mountains, huge ones."

The clerk turned around from the filing cabinet. "Yea. Lord, that John Stregal was smart. And charming. He could charm the bark off a tree."

"And nobody's been looking at this parcel?"

"Like I said, mister. No." The clerk turned back to his filing.

"Much obliged." Dawson stood and reached into a pocket. "Seek and ye shall find. Matthew 7:7-8." He put a Bible on the clerk's desk.

16

Olive lowered Georgia Ann into the crib and pulled a blanket over her tiny shoulders. She went to the bedroom doorway to listen for voices, a door closing, footsteps on the porch, movement of any kind, but quiet hung in the hall as heavy as a quilt. Olive inched back into the room and went to the dresser for a better look at the wedding photograph.

John stood next to his bride, one hand looped around her waist to rest lightly on her sash, white gloves in his other. He wore a black jacket the likes of which Olive had never seen, not even in a photograph, with its short, high lapels and tailored fit across his broad shoulders. A small spray of flowers sat on the right lapel, and she wanted it to have been pinned there by his mother, or a sister, or a servant, anyone but Annaliese. His eyes seemed joyless, vacant even, and she wondered if he was simply being formal for the photographer. She told herself that this joylessness had remained when he looked over at his bride after the photographer's flash. As for Annaliese, her expression was more relaxed. Olive pored over the details of her outfit, from her beribboned white dress to the slender bows on her silk shoes.

Olive had always known he was married, as the good ones always were, and that he was so many things she was not—educated, Catholic, urban, wealthy. These disparities added up to a man beyond her reach, but she had hoped. Once, she saw something in his eyes while he thrust himself inside her, or she thought so anyway. Over time, that image had latched on, taken root deep and strong in the fertile ground of her desperation.

Slowly, slowly she pulled open the top drawer and ran her hands lightly over sterling silver brushes, a boot hook, a mirror, and a nail file, but these were merely tools, nothing she coveted. She opened another drawer and her eyes lit up at silk and lace, embroidered collars, pin tucks, ruffles, and ribbons, stacks and stacks of it. Holding a camisole to her chest, she admired herself in the mirror, relished the way the softest white batiste she had ever touched turned her into someone else somehow, the someone she deserved to be. She returned the camisole to its folds. Opening another drawer, she gasped at the scent that hit her—John's scent. Shaving soap and shaving brushes lay beside his monogrammed handkerchiefs that were folded and stacked just so. She brought a brush to her nose and closed her eyes to savor him again.

The savoring nearly did her in, because she almost missed a shuffling sound downstairs. Quickly, her fingers ran through the handkerchiefs. Seven. Enough that one wouldn't be missed. She plucked one from the stack, rubbed it into the soap, left, right, up and down, and threw the soap back. She stuffed the handkerchief in her pocket and hurried downstairs.

Samuel rummaged through the shelves of the dark pantry.

She stood in the doorway and said, "You took some mending over to Ruth's cabin?"

The boy nodded as he stood on tiptoe and squinted at the shelves. "Applesauce?"

Olive reached for a jar on the shelf. "I've got it. Have a seat."

At the table, she spooned the applesauce into a bowl. "Glad to be back in Pinch?"

"Yes, ma'am." Samuel watched her sit down.

"What's the house at the lumber mill like? Big ol' white columns, grand dinin' room, lots of bedrooms?"

Samuel put a spoonful in his mouth, swallowed and said, "No, ma'am. No columns."

"Sorry about your pa."

The boy nodded into the bowl.

"He ever take you along when he went with the teams to cut the trees?"

"No, ma'am."

"Big boy like you? Never?"

His face crumpled a little.

She patted the boy's hand. "I'm glad to hear that. I mean, glad you wasn't there. I reckon it must've been an accident in the woods is how he died. A tree sprung back on him and cracked his skull? A branch clipped him comin' off the tree goin' down? They don't call them branches widow-makers for nothin'."

Samuel's mouth stopped moving.

"That's what happened, ain't it?"

"He died in the lumber mill. An accident with the saw."

Olive sat back in her chair. "A saw."

The boy's eyes were shimmering, but she thought she saw a kind of release there too, as though he was grateful to let the words out. "Uncle Ben too, his brother." When he didn't shy away from meeting her stare, she leaned in.

"They died in the same accident?" Olive asked.

Ruth appeared in the doorway at the hall. "That ain't none of your business," she said.

Olive stood and emptied the jar into the boy's bowl. With a pat to his shoulders, she went out the back door. Ruth followed her. "Hey! When did you say your baby was born?" she called.

"Couple months ago," Olive said over her shoulder. "Not that it's any of your business."

Watching her go, Ruth crossed her arms, relieved, but only on one point. Before he died in December, John Stregal hadn't left the county for about a year and a half. Once, Herschel had suggested that perhaps God had his hand at Olive's pitiful back, had steered her here for Annaliese's help as He had once steered them to Annaliese, and that Olive had nothing on her mind but survival. But Ruth knew she hadn't made a mistake about Olive's character. Money such as Annaliese's attracted the lowest of souls.

17

A bustling clump of women rushed at Herschel and Ruth as they emerged from the buggies and wagons scattered across the grounds of the Free Will Baptist Church. One of the women grabbed Lucy out of Ruth's arms and held the baby up to her three sisters, toothless all. The weekly scrutiny by Herschel's aunts that made Ruth's pulse race commenced. Lord, she prayed, let one of them say Lucy favors Herschel this week, even though she don't and never will.

Herschel's hopeful eyes followed the female faces flipping from him to the baby and back.

"Looky thar, at that mouth," an aunt said. "Don't that look like Herschel?"

Ruth's knees buckled. A smile creased Herschel's fair-skinned face as he grabbed his wife's elbow to steady her.

Another aunt squinted with piggy eyes that for fifty-eight years had picked through life in search of tragedy and injustice and said, "Naw, it don't, but next week she'll look like somebody else anyway." The woman lived to visit families of the recently departed, strangers mostly, and sit up all night with them while they exchanged startled glances.

Ruth scooped her baby out of the circle and hurried to church.

Inside, the morning light streamed in the unadorned windows of the small sanctuary to light the backs of ten rows of rough-hewn oak pews. Beneath the pulpit, the mourners' bench stretched out long and wide, the scene of epiphanies, declarations of salvation, confessions of adultery, and all manner of taking on during funerals. Stems of pink bee balm in a vase brightened the table next to the preacher's chair. The bearer of the vase had left a string of water spots all the way down the center aisle made of heart pine.

Herschel split off to sit with the men on the left. Ruth settled into a seat a few rows behind two women chatting quietly. She had made up her mind not to ask God anymore why He had let happen what happened to Miss Annaliese's baby. She wasn't going to ask, Didn't He hear her prayers for a safe birth and healthy baby? For a long while after the birth, she'd pictured those prayers lying on this floor, as inert as rocks, but eventually realized that Georgia Ann was, in fact, safely delivered and healthy, so Ruth blamed herself for not being more specific. Now, she had something else to talk to Him about. Ruth pressed the baby into her body and closed her eyes.

"Lord, forgive me for pestering you. Looks like Georgia Ann is growing jest fine. Seven and a half pounds yesterday on the scale," she prayed silently, "though we got to get her an operation before she starts tryin' to talk. So fer now I'm movin' on to something else and you know what it is. Please give me the strength to tell Herschel about this baby's true Pappy. It ain't right for me to keep this from him. I see him lookin' at her face so hard. I feel like my head's about to bust and the way Miss Annaliese is gettin' all wound up, I'm worried she's goin' to blurt it out soon."

The preacher started shuffling down the center aisle, nodding left and right at the flock, Bible tucked to chest. Ruth opened her eyes. Behind the preacher, a girl carried a cup of water, which she took to the pulpit. The preacher's wife in her usual black bonnet slipped in through a side door, so quiet and tiny she earned barely a glance, as she wished. Stragglers hurried to seats. Ruth watched a latecomer wave her three girls into a pew. Three yellow gingham bonnets came off, six coppery braids capped with yellow ribbons fell down little backs. Even in this world of without, mothers do what they can, Ruth thought.

She hurried through the rest of her prayer, explaining that had he known, Herschel would've beaten Mr. John to death, and she couldn't tell him after Mr. John died neither, for what was the point then? There was nothing worse for a man than raging at a ghost. Better to keep it to herself, she explained, and she thought Annaliese would too.

"But if she don't, Lord, I am such a fool," she whispered. "A fool and a liar all rolled up into one."

The preacher stepped up to the pulpit and cleared his throat to begin leading the men in reading Scripture aloud. Everyone stood in rigid attention, every hand held an open Bible, but the women's lips merely mouthed the passages they could say aloud only at home. After thirty minutes, the preacher stopped reading and everyone sat down. Throughout the reading, Ruth listened to God's thoughts on that choice she'd made.

After the service concluded, Ruth stood at the end of the pew to wait for Herschel to flow by with the men. "All right, Lord, I hear you," she whispered. "Tonight then. Hit's the right thing. I'll tell him tonight."

Herschel wrapped his papery hand around hers and took the basket holding his daughter. Ruth could barely breathe. Blood pulsed at the back of her eyes, blinding her to the floor, the door, the faces of friends waiting outside to say hello. Stepping into the sunshine, Ruth felt Herschel's hand was hotter than a skillet she might've pulled barehanded from the fire without thinking. She saw the friends coming closer. Were they moving toward her and Herschel, or were she and Herschel the ones in motion? Ruth was trying to focus when someone stepped in front of the three of them.

"Y'all ain't about to leave without me seein' her, is you?" asked a woman with a leathery face. "Ain't seen her since Sunday last."

"'Mornin' Aunt Pally," Herschel said, raising the basket obligingly.

Aunt Pally picked up the baby's feet and wiggled them. "Ain't you jest the prettiest little thang?"

With the flames of hell licking at her own feet, Ruth tried to take a step in the direction of the wagon she desperately wanted to get into, but Aunt Pally didn't move aside.

"Hold on," Aunt Pally said, leaning in for a closer look at the baby's toes. "Why, looky thar."

Hershel lifted the basket even higher. "What?" he asked.

"Them pinky toes. Each one has two freckles on it, jest like you had when you was a baby."

"Huh," Herschel said.

"What?" Ruth asked, leaning in.

"Mirror images. Two here and two there. Thought it was strange enough on you, Herschel, but now here it is again. Ain't that somethin'?" Aunt Pally let loose a cackle that brought people hurrying over. Ruth left the crowd for a shady spot under a tree. She watched their expressions as Pally explained her discovery and held up the toes. Some people shrugged, others shook their heads. Such a common thing, she heard them say. Every third person around here has red hair and freckles, someone said. She heard Herschel laugh like he hadn't in a long time. He kissed Lucy's toes. As the crowd broke up, he came for her, and the young family wove back through the buggies and wagons, one parent feeling particularly light-headed.

18

The Pinch schoolhouse, perched at the crown of a hill, looked down upon the town's personalities that had been molded inside its four walls, some more forcefully than others. Weathered pine steps worn down by generations of foot draggers rose from the broom-swept dirt yard. Inside, Annaliese and Emeline stood at a cabinet, shelving supplies handed to them by Corinthia Meddling.

Corinthia pulled a gray slate framed in wood out of the box. "I never reckoned I'd see these purty things in my classroom," she said. "A whole case of 'em. Sure do appreciate this."

Annaliese nodded as she handed a package of slate pencils to Emeline.

"Any of them children screak them pencils on these slates, I'll be takin' a hickory switch to some legs," Corinthia said.

At this mention of switching, Emeline looked up at her mother with alarm. Her brother's calves still bore scars from a teacher who'd gone to the bushes to break off a strip of hickory and come back to deliver mountain-style punishment with gusto, a teacher long gone and never in this room that was Corinthia's domain, but for the little girl soon to begin school, a scary pattern was emerging.

Annaliese patted Emeline's shoulder. "Maybe sometimes the children don't mean to do that."

Corinthia gave her a weary look.

"Maybe some of the children are—" Annaliese disliked the word idiot, though its use was common enough. The 1900 census takers who had come to her house had asked if there were any idiots in the family. "Slow," she said.

"You mean like Augustus Bell," Corinthia said.

"Yes, exactly," Annaliese said. "I heard that when he was a toddler, a chimney fell on him."

"Chimbley musta fell on the whole damn family then," Corinthia muttered.

With a smile, Annaliese looked around the room littered with empty boxes and desks. "Where are the Blueback Spellers?"

"At the post office. Couldn't carry everything at once."

"I'll get them," Annaliese said as she stood up to stretch her back.

"I'm going with you," Emeline said with a panicked glance at Corinthia.

"Now, honey, you stay and help Miss Meddling. I'll be right back."

Emeline grabbed her mother's skirt.

"That's fine, Mrs. Stregal," Corinthia said. "I've got rosters to put together. I'll see y'all in a little while."

Annaliese and Emeline walked hand in hand down to the railroad tracks where the black crown of a locomotive had just cut them off from town. Open freight cars thundered past, loaded to the limits of their steel arms with logs. Emeline clamped her hands over her ears. Annaliese shaded her eyes to look down the track at the long dark line of shuddering carriages that had no end. Car after car raced by, each one full of trees that had stood for centuries until yesterday, the columns of nature's cathedrals. Annaliese kept counting, twenty, twenty-five, thirty cars. In a sickening rhythm, they clicked and clacked along the rails, taking the mountains' glory to their fate as paneling, windowsills, and floors in bloated Newport mansions. Finished poplar took paint too beautifully. Oak made floors that were too strong. Finally, the last car swept by. Annaliese couldn't bring herself to look at it. She picked up her daughter's hand and took off with too much speed for Emeline's little legs.

As they passed the post office, Emeline said nothing, having been delivered from evil and hoping to keep it that way.

Annaliese found Henry at the bank, recognizing the back of his head and shoulders at the teller's cage. They waited for him in the soothing cool of the marble lobby. The floor, a wash of snow laced with rivulets of gray, radiated calm and perhaps even the slightest bit of a chill, not unlike the building's two bankers—grounded, immovable, reassuringly boring. Churches and their keepers are that way too, Annaliese thought. People like the most important institutions of their lives to be as immutable as mountains. Banks. City Halls. Hospitals. Universities. But there were no institutions in the lumber business, the least organized of all industries. In the lumber business, as in the woods, anything could happen. People took out guns on one another over land disputes. Moonshiners burned homes and barns after loggers stumbled across their stills. Monied and glorified men cheated one another in shipments and contracts. Thanks to John, who ran an ethical operation and railed against those who didn't, Annaliese understood the underworld all too well.

The more calcified of the two bank officers, Mr. Bedney Loomis, crossed the lobby with a man who wore a tailor-made suit and waistcoat. Annaliese noted that the stranger's black button-up boots were smooth and shiny, and his gray beard clearly was attended to daily by scissors. The two men, heads bent together in conversation, didn't notice her until they were almost at the door. Annaliese tried to hide behind a column, but Loomis was having none of that when it came to one of his biggest depositors.

"Ah, Mrs. Stregal, good day. So good to see you out and about again." The banker smiled down upon Emeline then back at her mother. "Something I could help you with?"

"A pleasure to see you, Mr. Loomis. No, nothing thank you," Annaliese said.

His companion looked her over as if she were on display in the Smith's Mercantile window. His eyes traveled over the round hips and high bosom that even her mourning dress couldn't diminish. He turned toward Loomis to be introduced.

"Where are my manners? Mrs. John Stregal, I'd like to introduce you to Mr. Charles Widener of Philadelphia," Loomis said.

Annaliese hadn't missed the man's vulgar scan of her body. "Mr. Widener," she said with a stiff nod. She didn't offer her hand.

Widener tugged on his lapels. "Mrs. Stregal," he said. "A pleasure."

"Mr. Widener is a munitions dealer. His father made their money in the Civil War," Loomis said.

Widener put up his hands. "He sold to both sides, let me just say," he said with a wink.

She could see him looking for appeasement or amusement on her face, but she made certain he found neither.

"He just bought thirty thousand acres along the Cartecay River," Loomis said.

"I've got restless money," Widener laughed. "Looking to invest my eggs in different baskets, shall we say. Everyone in my club back home has been eyeing the South."

"Mrs. Stregal's husband was in the lumber industry," Loomis said with a dip toward her.

"Ah, yes, Stregal Brothers Lumber Company," Widener said. "Good reputation. So you'll be selling the company?"

"Thank you for your condolences, sir," Annaliese said with a tincture of disdain.

Loomis winced.

"My apologies, ma'am," the man said, but his eyes still held the question.

"No. Not selling," Annaliese said. Please, she thought, do not offer me honeyed bromides about John's reputation and your implication that I mustn't let it decline.

Emeline pulled her hand out of her mother's crushing grip.

The two men stared at Annaliese. Finally, Loomis said, "Oh, wait. Of course. Your brother-in-law has come back to town. He'll be running the company then?" He wiggled his shoulders with pride over his insight.

"So you can tend to this little one here," Widener said, patting Emeline's head.

"Quite right. The domestic sphere," Loomis said.

Annaliese was trying to put together a memorable reply to deliver just before flipping her skirt and swishing out the door when she saw Henry approaching. While the men exchanged introductions and pleasantries, Henry kept snatching looks at her stony face. The conversation flowed into Widener's bragging and Loomis' hints about the size of the deposit Widener had just made, until even Henry was inching toward the door, hand extended for Annaliese and Emeline to go first.

"Gentlemen, good day," Henry said over his shoulder.

Outside, Annaliese stormed down the sidewalk. Emeline hurried to keep up again. "That's it," Annaliese said. "Henry, that's absolutely it."

19

The Stregal Brothers Lumber Company mill was deep in the hills of Gilmer County, a two-hour wagon ride from Pinch when roads were dry, which they were on the May day that Annaliese and her family returned. Annaliese rode next to Henry in the first of four wagons loaded with family and provisions. Georgia Ann, four weeks old, rocked along in her arms. Two horses tied to the wagons trotted behind, ears up and eyes bright with curiosity.

They rolled into the lumberyard just as the sawmill's noon whistle pierced the air, as though there were still dozens of laboring sawyers in the mill listening for break time. There was only the skeleton crew of eight, and they were already taking a break outside, had been all week. They leaned on the corral fence where the mules had marshaled to see what the four wagons were about. Annaliese forced herself to look at the sawmill, the last place where the father of the baby in her arms had been alive. Three months since she'd looked at it last and still her heart raced at the sight. Henry, no less shaky, put his arm around her shoulder. She patted his hand to signal that she knew he was jolted too. She looked over the other buildings clustered in the red clay bowl that had been gouged out of the forest—the planing mill, the dry kiln, the commissary, the office, and the vast drying yard where manufactured lumber had once stood in towering stacks. Everything looked the same.

The office door flew open, and Wade practically ran at the wagons.

While she hadn't expected the crew to be lined up in two columns, hats held at their sides, as they were when she returned to bury John on a nearby hillside, she had expected them to get off the fence at least. No one moved. The eight were a tableau of insolence. She handed the baby to Henry, smoothed her pants with sweaty hands, and jumped out of the wagon.

Wade met her halfway. They shook hands and spoke for a minute, and although she didn't trust her legs, she turned around and headed for the fence with her hand held out to force the men to come down and shake it. The eyes above their long, riotous beards were guarded, but each accepted her hand, a few of them mumbling "Hello, ma'am" or "Welcome back" in gravely voices. She shook the gnarly hands with as much authority as she could muster, flinching every time she ran into a missing finger or thumb. Body stench came off them heavy and sour—a source of pride for a mountain man, she knew, for it said *I'm a working man*. One could say the Scots-Irish were stiff-necked, but never that they were afraid of hard work. She knew these men dynamited splash dams and wrestled slippery logs from the millpond into the mill, shoved them into ten-foot band saws, and worked ten-hour days in the brutal sawmill. They had worked hard for John, she had to give them that. But that was John.

The men went back to their slouching on the fence to watch her hurry back to the wagon for the last of the journey uphill to the two white houses. The sight of the excited children in the wagon made her smile. Tension drained from her body as she climbed in beside Henry. Two things she'd been dreading—the sight of the sawmill and the shaking of hands—were over, and now she was on her way to her beloved home, where tonight candlelight would dance again in those dark windows.

The geese that owned the place swarmed down the hill at the wagons, hissing and threatening with black beaks. Samuel exploded out of the wagon to run at them.

"Show off!" Emeline shouted. As soon as the exhausted horses stopped at the houses and the geese had scattered, she jumped out and ran toward

Ruth's cabin in back. Olive followed slowly, watching for the geese to loop back. Annaliese called for her to stop, for the baby was rooting and restless, but she was gone.

"I know, I know," she said to the baby as she climbed the steps. "We'll get you fed in a minute. Come see your home, Georgie." On the porch sat one large and two small rocking chairs coated in yellow pollen. "Hush now, look," Annaliese said. With joy, she pushed open the door.

The foyer, smaller than she remembered, smelled of long ago fires. Annaliese stepped onto the parquet floors that John was so proud of when he first led her inside, all energy and chatter. To compensate for the home she'd left behind in Louisville, he lined this hall with oak wainscoting and hand-carved crown molding. North Carolina artisans had hammered oak and walnut strips into the intricate pattern on the floor. In the parlor and dining room there were oak-paneled walls, oak spandrels, and oak carvings. No indoor plumbing but this, she thought when she first saw it all. Moving deeper inside, her boot found the first sweet creak in the floor. She showed the baby the doorway where Samuel had penciled his growth, the parlor with shrouded furniture, and the dining room with tall leather chairs that had been wiped down and the table set for supper.

Henry arrived at the front door with the kitchen scale. "Upstairs or kitchen?" he asked.

A woman came running down the hall with arms out for Annaliese.

"Minerva," Annaliese cried.

"You're home," Minerva said. She flapped long, loose-jointed arms as she came. Strands of auburn hair flew in all directions.

Annaliese gave her a one-armed hug and introduced the baby who was mashed between them.

Ruth called to them from the kitchen doorway at the end of the hall. "Y'all gotta see this."

Dishes of food lined the kitchen table. Tin pans covered with greasy dishtowels suggested fried chicken beneath, or potatoes, or beans. Two lattice-crust pies oozed purple juice. Samuel and Emeline slipped their hands into a basket of biscuits. Beside the table stood a baby high chair made of crooked tree limbs and the woven roots of the huckleberry bush. Its seat held a cushion made of plaited cloth remnants, red, green, and yellow.

"Minerva," Annaliese cried again. "You did all this?"

"No, ma'am," Minerva said. She tilted her head to the back door. "You just missed them."

Annaliese pushed it open.

Four women and a string of children walked toward the forested slope, empty baskets in hands. One of the children looked back, pulled on her mother's hand, and when everyone turned, Annaliese saw that they were the wives and sisters of the sawyers, the mothers of children in the school Annaliese had built in the mountains. A woman raised an arm to her— Sarah, who two years ago had had no chickens to fry, no coats or shoes for her eight children. Beside her stood Hattie, whose shelves were so bare that the family ate frogs and eels, even turtles. When Stregal Brothers Lumber Company arrived, rare cash did too, delivering chickens, eggs, canned Alaskan salmon, coats, sewing machines that enabled the women to earn cash of their own, and sugar for the pies they could now afford to share.

She raised an arm in thanks and held Georgia up to introduce her. They waved before turning back to the forest.

Seated at the head of her dining room table where so many happy memories had been made, Annaliese savored the sight of her family and Henry settling once again into the chairs. She made the sign of the cross, which triggered the same around the table with Dorothy, Phillip, Samuel, and Emeline. Henry, the Baptist at the other end of the table, closed his eyes and bowed his head. In the doorway to the kitchen, Herschel and Ruth bowed their heads as well. Olive crossed her arms and watched.

"Heavenly Father," Annaliese said. "We thank you for this day of homecoming, this bounteous meal, and the loving hands that prepared it. These gifts of your generous earth sustain our bodies, your grace sustains our souls. Your love opens our eyes to realize the talents you have bestowed upon us. Let us remember our responsibility to steward this precious earth, to take care of our neighbors, lettered and not, and to use our talents as you intend. Let us see in every person your face, in every cathedral forest your hand."

Dorothy opened her eyes to look at her sister, generally not one to go beyond the rote. She caught Phillip doing the same.

"Golly, Mama," Samuel said. In eight years of listening to grace at her table, he had never heard such fervor before.

Annaliese kept her eyes closed. "And please, God, do not let me make a small fortune out of a large fortune with Stregal Brothers Lumber Company. In the name of the Father, the Son, and the Holy Ghost. Amen."

"Amen," Henry said heartily.

"And Lord," Phillip said. "Grant us some degree of fortune for the herbal medicine business we've come here to start."

"Amen," Dorothy said.

Olive remained unusually still, quietly watching the Catholics and their ritual.

Hands reached for serving spoons and passed the basket of biscuits. Forks and knives got busy. Ruth had to poke Olive to life to get her to help with refilling empty platters. As Annaliese felt her body warming with the food, she looked around the dining room again. Cobwebs draped between the sconces and dusty oak panels, but soon enough the panels would be wiped and oiled so that candlelight could again light up their rings of gold. The photographs and clocks would be unpacked and placed on shelves, all of them soon to be coated with the inevitable sawdust that would be floating up the hill.

Then there was Henry. He caught her dreamy look and returned it with such a long look of contentment that she wondered if he was saying, Look at us appearing marital, with you at one end of the family table and me at the other. If I were the husband I appear to be, I would be sleeping upstairs tonight with you instead of next door at Dorothy and Phillip's house.

Don't be silly, Annaliese told herself. Henry isn't thinking that. What on earth had come over her to make her think that he would? Perhaps this honeyed warmth sweeping over her was simply the happy children at the table and the soothing embrace of the familiar room. But the longer she lingered on Henry's gaze, the wider his eyes grew. Dorothy noticed and elbowed Phillip.

After supper, while the women were washing dishes, Olive banged pots and slammed cabinet doors.

At the sink, Dorothy whispered to Ruth, "What's that all about?"

Ruth handed her a dish to dry. "She's riled up over that cot in the hall for her."

"But there are only three bedrooms upstairs. What did she expect?"

"She thought she'd get a real bed and her own room. Says she thought this house was going to be big and fancy."

Olive inserted herself into the whispering. "And no indoor plumbing neither," she said. "With all of his money? It's a long way out there to that crapper." Her volume rose with each word.

Ruth shot a look at Dorothy that said the true Olive had arrived.

Annaliese came in from the hall. "Bridle your tongue, Mrs. Washburn."

Olive took off her apron, slapped it against the table, and headed for the back door. "I'm going for a walk," she said.

No one offered her a lantern.

"Be back in an hour," Annaliese said. "The baby will be hungry."

20

Union County, Georgia

Buck Dawson closed in on the slope that the mountaineer had pointed out. For days Dawson had combed through the mountains looking at the scattered parcels owned by the Stregal Brothers Lumber Company. Finally, sixty miles from Pinch, he found a man who knew the poplars Dawson was describing, tulip trees the man called them, in stands so dense that the forest floor was dark at noon. Over in Union County on Hickory Mountain.

Dawson gripped the reins at the sight, which was no exaggeration on the part of the mountaineer. The thick canopies crowded out the sunshine. He entered the sparse understory easily. He passed huge trees, nine feet wide at breast height and more than 180 feet tall, literally the kings of the forest. The leaf litter was undisturbed, and lateral tree branches at horse-height were unbroken. Other timber cruisers had not been here yet, but they'd be coming. Dawson started counting as far as he could see.

When he figured he'd seen the last of them, he topped a ridge and saw that the kings rolled on for fifty more acres. As evening shadows fell, Dawson set up a tent under the canopies. He fed his horse and ran his hands along her loin and rump, then moved down to the gaskins, hocks, and cannons to check for gashes or swellings. Satisfied, he stroked her velvet muzzle, and she closed her eyes as if she sensed his gratitude for bringing him to this treasure. He built a fire but cooked nothing to heed the mountaineer's warning about the mountain panthers. Whiskey, though, he wouldn't deny himself that on this glorious occasion. He read his Bible by the firelight as long as he could. By the time he closed his bleary eyes, he had estimated more than two-hundred-forty-thousand board feet and a net of about $10,000 from hundreds of poplars that he was betting that the widow Stregal didn't even know she owned.

21

The roosters had been up for hours, so the adults of the two households were dressed and cupping their coffee in Annaliese's kitchen at six o'clock. Annaliese nodded at each chore being discussed, but she was barely there, exhausted from a night of shaking Olive awake and keeping an eye on her to make sure she finished the feeding. She wanted to leave her baby to the woman and go back to sleep, but she couldn't.

After breakfast, Annaliese walked Henry out the front door. He dropped his saddlebags to the ground to take her hands. "I'll see you Friday. Hoyt's train gets in late Thursday," he said.

"Thank God he's willing to come back. He's the only employee those stumpers ever listened to."

He pulled her closer. "Not sure I want to leave you up here."

Annaliese lifted a shoulder toward the house. "My rifle's already hung over the front door," she said with a laugh.

Henry shook his head. "You know what I mean."

She raised her hand to stroke the smoothness of his freshly shaved cheeks. Just as the scent of his soap whispered past her, Samuel and Emeline ran out of the house. The adults dropped their hands. The children threw their arms around Henry's knees. After enough head-patting and farewells, Henry climbed on his horse and rode away.

Annaliese and the children waved long after he'd stopped looking back.

While Herschel and Phillip disappeared to do the kinds of mystery jobs that require men to go missing until supper, the women swept the floors clean of mice and their droppings, grit and pollen, spiders dead and alive. Rugs were hung and beaten in the blinding sunshine, furniture coverings folded away, all surfaces wiped down with rags and buckets of water. Ruth made room in the pantry for the kitchen scale among the sacks, cans, and barrels. Olive moved from room to room, making her annoyance clear each time someone disturbed her feeding or diapering.

After the mid-day meal, Annaliese and Dorothy sat in the parlor to open boxes and return things to mantel and shelves. As Dorothy unwrapped a square package, she ran her hands over it slowly and then held it up to her sister.

In the black-and-white photograph, John and Samuel stood in front of the enormous Stregal Brothers Lumber Company sign on the side of the mill. John's hands rested on his son's shoulders.

"We should put at least one photograph of him out," Dorothy said.

Annaliese remembered taking that photograph and the way Samuel had leaned back into his father, relaxed and proud. That moment had been a good one, a time when the children still welcomed his hands on them. She nodded as Dorothy placed it on the table beside the settee, and went back to her unpacking.

Ruth came to the door to announce a fresh pot of coffee and ginger cakes coming out of the oven. At the kitchen table, Annaliese asked where Olive and the children were. Georgia was asleep upstairs but would be hungry soon. Ruth answered that the children were up the hill at the chicken coop but she hadn't seen Olive for hours. Ruth put Lucy to her breast, and as expected, the sound of Georgia Ann's crying floated downstairs.

Annaliese went out the back door to look for Olive. Nothing stirred around Ruth and Herschel's cabin or the chicken coop, except for the children chasing a flurry of yellow chicks. The outhouse door stood open. The stable seemed empty. Annaliese came back inside and pumped water into a pan, put it on the warm stovetop, and pulled a jar out of the icebox. Her thin, near-blue breast milk filled only a few inches of the Mason jar.

"Dorothy, would you please see if you can find her?" Annaliese asked as she put the jar in the pan.

By the time Annaliese got the last drop into Georgia Ann, she could hear the argument in the yard. Dorothy dragged Olive inside. Olive's white blouse, open to the waist, was streaked with red dirt. She clutched at it clumsily, as if she was embarrassed in front of the three women, though the leaves clinging to her hair and skirt suggested modesty was the last thing on her mind a few minutes ago.

"I found her down at the sawmill with one of the sawyers," Dorothy said, letting go of Olive's arm.

Ruth closed the door.

"We was jest gettin' to the good part," Olive said with slurred speech. "Then she showed up, damn it."

"How could you?" Annaliese asked. She put Georgia Ann in a basket near the sink.

"Well, you ain't got nothing else to offer 'round here," Olive said.

"You have wages, don't you?" Annaliese asked.

"Ain't seen no money yet," Olive said.

"I said I'd pay you when we got settled up here."

Olive staggered toward Annaliese. "No, you're gonna pay right now."

"What does that mean?" Annaliese asked.

"What do you want?" Dorothy asked

"Well, it's more like what do *you* want?" Olive asked. "I'll tell you. You want me to keep my mouth shut."

The three other women went very still.

"I knew your husband," Olive said with a sway of the hips.

"You already said you met him at the cotton mill," Ruth said.

"Oh, no, I mean I *knew* him." Olive laughed. "You know—like the Bible kind of knew."

Annaliese couldn't breathe. Was this possible? John had been in Canton only once, about three years ago as far as she knew. Had he returned? Three years ago, John was a well man and no cheater.

Olive smoothed her hand over the dimples of the tin tabletop and waited.

Dorothy looked at her sister for outrage, denial—something!—but Annaliese was silent. A crimson flush raced up her neck. "You're lying," Annaliese finally said.

"Oh, no I ain't. John and me, we had something special. He loved me. After you came to Georgia, he couldn't come to me no more, but he sent a man to my door with an envelope every couple months. One hunnert whole dollars each time," Olive said with a thrust of her chest. "Few months ago, the man stopped comin'. When the obituary got passed around the spinnin' room, I knew what happened. Then the money run out. You and me, we're goin' to talk."

John's shaving brushes pushed to the side in a jumble in my drawer, thought Annaliese. A snake rifling through my bedroom, holding my newborn.

"This is ridiculous," Dorothy said. "John would never—"

"Get out of my house," Annaliese said in a steely whisper.

Olive leaned forward. "I can tell you pert near ever thing about his privates, like them tiny red spots on his balls, swollen and purple as ripe figs."

"For heaven's sake, that proves nothing," Dorothy said.

"Then there's the way he liked to have his nipples pulled on."

Ruth put her hand to her throat.

Annaliese's face went white. "Stop," she said.

Olive pointed her finger. "See there? You know what I'm gettin' at. How he loved to have them pinched and twisted. I swear them things was strung right down to his pecker. That's sure enough strange, and what's more, there's that thing he said in some kind of gibberish in my ear right when he come. Mudder something. Bam!" Olive slapped her hands together and laughed.

"I said stop." Annaliese backed away to stand in front of the basket where Georgia Ann slept.

Dorothy looked at her sister with growing confusion.

"Get out," Annaliese said again.

"Sure will, right after we settle up with five hunnert dollars," Olive said.

Ruth rushed to Annaliese's side.

"Or I'll tell," Olive said. "Mrs. Stregal, high and mighty, had a cheatin' husband."

"Ruth, go get my bank drafts folder," Annaliese said.

"Anna! No!" Dorothy said.

Ruth ran down the hall with Lucy.

Seconds later, Annaliese ripped a signed check out of the folder. "Now you listen to me," she said, handing over the check. "Here's two hundred for what you've done for my baby, three times what I owe you. Take it or leave it. Tomorrow at first light, Herschel will take you to the train station. Go to Atlanta or Chattanooga or wherever—I don't care—but I never want to hear from you again."

Olive pushed away from the table, defiance shining in her eyes, and came over to clamp her finger and thumb on the check.

"And you'll keep your mouth shut," Annaliese said, not letting go.

Olive nodded and Annaliese released the check. Olive shouldered her way out the back door.

Annaliese collapsed against the sink. Dorothy grabbed her wrist. "Why did you pay her? She's lying," she said.

Ruth came over to put her hand lightly on Dorothy's grip.

"He wouldn't do such a thing," Dorothy said.

Annaliese looked into her sister's irises, gray and blue shards under glass. "Yes, Dottie, he would." The column of air inside their circle went cold. "Ruth's child," Annaliese said.

"Lucy?" Dorothy said, swiveling to the baby asleep in Ruth's arms. "Lucy is John's child?"

"It ain't what you think," Ruth said. Her eyes pleaded with Annaliese to get on with it, to lay bare what John had done to her. She and Annaliese had never discussed how they would handle telling anyone. They never thought they would have to.

"It wasn't Ruth's fault," Annaliese said.

"Rape?" Dorothy asked. "Not John."

"Dottie, you of all people know he was capable of that," Annaliese said. "Remember what you heard behind our bedroom door one night? My bruises after?"

"But he was so clearly mad by then. With Olive, that would've been almost three years ago."

"I realized a long time ago how good he was at hiding his illness."

"But cheating?"

Annaliese raised her hands. "I didn't think he'd jump on a log headed for a bandsaw and slice himself to bits either, Dottie."

Dorothy reared back, then put her hand on her sister's arm. "Oh, Anna, I'm sorry." She took a sideways glance at Ruth. "I'm so sorry for you, too."

Ruth pressed her baby to her chest. Glistening ribbons of tears tracked down her cheeks.

"And you mean to tell me you and Ruth have made peace with this?" Dorothy asked.

Ruth watched Annaliese's face.

"What choice do we have? Everyone here is innocent. John's gone. No one else knows," Annaliese said.

"Not even Herschel?" Dorothy asked.

"Especially not Herschel," Ruth said with some heat.

Though she hadn't missed that heat, Dorothy plunged on. "But, how do you know he's not the father?"

"No baby for the year before Mr. John jumped me," Ruth said, "and ain't been no baby since."

"That's because you're still nursing," Dorothy whispered.

Annaliese put her hand on Dorothy's arm. "Dottie. Stop. It's done."

The women went quiet to let pulses settle. Finally, Ruth said, "I've got to change a nappy."

That night, Annaliese tried to rush the children to bed. In her bedroom, Ruth worked on expressing her milk and dribbling it into Georgia Ann. Outside, the sound of frogs rose in waves, *mezzo forte* and *mezzo piano*. Farther away, distant canyons rumbled with the dying cadences of thunder.

"It's good to be home," Samuel said, as his mother smoothed the fresh sheet across his chest. A drawing the boy had made of his father and him on a river raft hung from a nail over his bed.

Annaliese turned away from it. "Time to go to sleep, Sam."

"Remember our first night here? When we were afraid of the sounds outside? The foxes we heard?"

"Yes, honey, I remember."

"And the dark. So dark. No streetlamps." Samuel looked outside.

A full moon, as luminescent and plump as a pearl, hung low in the sky, spreading silver light on every resting blade and bough. But this calm scene did not bring Annaliese peace.

"Read to us, Mama?" Emeline said from the other bed. She got up on her elbows and looked hopefully around the room at the unopened crates.

"Not tonight, Emmie."

Emeline lay back down. "Just the four of us here now in this house, Mama?"

"'Course, Emmie," Samuel said with authority. "Miss Olive is going to sleep in the room above the stable out back."

"No, she's leaving tomorrow," Annaliese said.

"Why?"

"She doesn't like it here," Annaliese said.

Emeline wiggled down into her bed. "Why isn't Miss Olive feeding Georgia tonight?"

Annaliese kissed Samuel and moved over to her daughter's bed. "No more questions, Emmie. Please."

Out in the hall, Dorothy was pacing.

"Miss Olive was mean tonight," Emeline said.

"Meaner'n usual," Samuel said. "She pushed me down on her way to the stable."

"Are you all right?" Annaliese asked.

"Sure."

"Aunt Dorothy and Uncle Phillip are going to live next door in Aunt Lucenia's house?" Emeline asked.

"Yes."

"How long?"

"A long time. Now hush. Close your eyes." Annaliese kissed her daughter's forehead and lowered the kerosene flame to a nub.

"Why is Aunt Dottie walking up and down the hall so loud?" Emeline asked.

Annaliese said nothing.

"What about prayers?" Emeline asked. "We didn't say prayers."

Annaliese threw her arm over her eyes. "Emeline Marie Stregal."

The girl fell quiet, and when Annaliese looked down at her, she saw that the look in her eyes had changed.

With another sigh, Annaliese lifted the edge of her quilt, nudged her over, and slipped in. Samuel leaned over to take his mother's hand. Together, they filled the darkness with the prayers they knew by heart, two times through then three, until Emeline's body grew heavy and Samuel's hand fell away.

When Annaliese closed the door, Dorothy's pointed at the stairs and started down. Annaliese looked in on the baby that was humped over Ruth's shoulder, lifeless as a sack of rice.

In the parlor, the sisters sat knee to knee on the settee—twelve and fourteen years old again, whispering, embarrassed.

"Well?" Dorothy asked.

"Where's Phillip?" Annaliese asked.

"Next door."

Annaliese turned back from her scan of the hallway. "She's right."

"The nipples business."

"Yes."

"So what. Maybe it's common."

"What about Phillip? Does he like that?"

"Oh, Anna. In bed, you could pull on a man's anything, an ear, an elbow and he would—"

Annaliese hushed her.

"All right, but I thought you wanted to know about Phillip. I can't believe we're talking about this."

"Well, we are. What about the tiny red spots? Does Phillip have red spots? There?"

Dorothy pulled in a long breath. "I have no idea."

"Oh."

"But come on. That could be a heat rash."

"But he had them." Annaliese ran her hand down the settee's velour and back, scraping channels of light and dark purple with her fingers. "Then there's the other thing."

"The gibberish."

"Yes."

"Mudder something, she said."

"What does Phillip say? At that moment?" Annaliese asked.

"Nothing."

"No words?"

"Just grunts. What are you getting at? John used to say something?"

"Yes."

"Well?"

"Mater Dei."

Dorothy straightened. "Mater Dei?"

Annaliese hushed her again. "Phillip's never said that? Not even once?"

Dorothy squinted at her sister. "Called out 'Mother of God' in Latin?" She shook her head in astonishment.

Annaliese stared through her tears at her sister's face, a cauldron of confusion, disgust, disbelief. "In Canton, Georgia, how many men, all Baptists and Methodists surely, would even know any Latin?" she asked.

"The language of the hated Papists," Dorothy finished.

"All I need is one," Annaliese said. "One other man in Canton, Georgia who would know those words."

22

As soon as Herschel's wagon rumbled away with Olive, Annaliese pried open the wooden crate that held the contents of her bedroom bureau. She dug through undergarments and stockings to pull out John's shaving brushes and handkerchiefs. She found the monogrammed drawstring lingerie bag—pearlized beads and trapunto lilies sewn onto white satin—that was part of her trousseau. Into the bag went John's handkerchiefs, his shaving brushes, his shaving soap, and anything that smelled of his shaving soap. The wedding photo in its silver-crusted frame went in too, and she yanked the string taut.

Annaliese flew out the back door for the stable. Minutes later, shovel in hand, she headed for the well-worn path behind the house. It was an uphill climb for a few minutes, but the way was clear, and soon she saw the tops of the red cedars rising above the hill. Annaliese paused at her sister-in-law's headstone, the first of three standing in the cedars' scented embrace. It read:

Lucenia Hopewell Stregal
loving wife and mother
October 1, 1868 – September 8, 1902.

"Lucenia," Annaliese whispered. "Can you believe him?"

She threw the silk bag down on the blanket of leaves and cedar needles atop John's grave. The first slam of the shovel shattered the photograph's glass into satisfying tinkles. Over and over she hammered the bag with the flat side down, then sideways to chop and pierce. As the bag tore, a shaving brush flew out, and she went after it until it slid into the ground in three pieces. Back at the bag, the soap popped out and became slivers, the photograph became pulp. Finally, she dug a wild hole, throwing the dirt over her back but mostly onto it, and pushed everything in, cursing him all the while. The white silk bag disappeared, its filthy ribbons trailing behind it on their pathetic way into the darkness. She scraped dirt to cover the hole and pounded it beyond flat, beyond reason, rattling John's bones in their airless, black space. With each slam, she ached to be as ignorant as she had been the day before when she hadn't heard the words that were now seared into her brain. *Mater Dei.* Something the ill-educated Olive couldn't have guessed.

On her way back down the hill, she saw Ruth and the mule plowing through last year's garden. Her hands and commands flew at the mule, a lazy animal known to loop back to start the next row before finishing the previous. Before they'd left Pinch, Ruth had said that mid-May was late for starting a garden, but people would say she was lazy if she didn't put one in, so she was putting one in. She didn't have time to wait to plant by the signs neither, she said, so she'd be calling it her By the Grace of God garden. Emeline danced along the edges of the action, brown and barefoot. Samuel strode beside them with Lucy in a ,sling across his chest, a sight that tightened the knot in Annaliese's stomach. The children were giddy over the worms boiling up, the bullets of mud slinging from the mule's hooves, and Ruth's slapping the reins. Samuel saw his mother, waved with glee. Annaliese ran to the house to release another round of tears.

Collecting herself at the kitchen sink, she smoothed a dishtowel on the counter more times that it needed and hung it on the rack below. She checked on Georgia Ann upstairs with Dorothy, kissed them both, and headed for the front door. Tucking a leather bag under her arm, she walked down the hill to the company office where Wade waited for her.

The mill yard was alive with the sawmill hands making a lively show of initiative as they sharpened tools again, swept out the sawmill, and brushed down the mules. Taking a deep breath, she walked through the office door.

Along the far wall of the office, two oak desks cleared of papers and the usual sawdust faced each other. A row of wooden filing cabinets lined the opposite dingy wall where a calendar hung askew on a nail. On a shelf, the company's leather-bound ledgers had been straightened into tidy stacks. John's black iron safe, as tall as a sixteen-hand horse, stood under a dusty windowsill.

Wade pulled out the chair at what was now her desk. She set the bag down and smoothed her hands as far as she could across it. Head down, she remained silent and still, seemingly focused on the whorls of wood grain. Then she straightened, crossed herself, opened the bag and pulled out an inkwell made of amber glass that looked like a perfume bottle with its delicate silver collar and etched footer. With slow, deliberate movement that implied forethought, she placed it at the right corner. Next came the fountain pen, collared with the same engraved silver, which she placed beside the inkwell. Finally, a crystal glass bowl was brought out and placed to her left. Sunshine ignited blues and golds in its facets. She opened a box of paper clips and poured them in.

The handoff began. They went over ledgers, letters, invoices, and expired contracts. The inventory outside was worthless, as anyone could see from the warped stacks in the mill yard, and the generator needed parts. She groaned at the outrageous payroll amount. Wade reminded her that John had doubled the sawyers' pay just before he died. It wasn't Wade's place to change it.

"You would've had a riot out there if you had," she said. "I'll have a word with the men about this."

"Mr. Henry going to be here for that?" Wade asked.

Annaliese made a face. "Now, Wade, I can do that by myself."

Wade shoved his hands in his pockets.

"They knew John wasn't right in the head," she said. "They know they've been taking advantage."

Wade crossed the room to the safe and reached for the ring of keys on top. "There's five hundred cash in here and all the important papers." Wade shook the ring and pinched one key to hold out to her. "This one here's to the safe. Mr. John kept all the legal documents, contracts, titles, anything important in there."

She looked over at the huge safe, big as an ox, hulking below the window, John's usual overkill.

A knock came at the door. At the sound of Annaliese's call, Minerva stuck her head in. "Ready when you are," she said to Wade. "My saddlebags are packed."

Annaliese stood up. "Missing your home, I'm sure," she said. She went to the door to hug the woman and thank her for taking care of her home.

Wade went for his hat on the coat rack. "By the way, some man came by a few days ago wantin' to know if you wanted to sell some of your land. I told him to talk to you when you was back and settled. Figured you'd say no."

"Did you get his name?"

"Dawson. Buck Dawson." Wade pulled his hat on. "Mr. Henry and Hoyt are comin' in later today?"

Annaliese smiled. "It's all right, Wade. You can go. Yes, they'll be here before nightfall." She shooed him toward the door. "Go on now. Don't keep your wife waiting."

"When y'all go timber cruising, I'd like to come to learn a few things from this forester you been talking about."

"Of course."

"Anything you need, you let me know."

"I will. Thank you again."

Wade started out the door, hesitated. He backed up and said, "Miss Annaliese, you and me, we been through a lot. All them pine trees we planted to make up for what Mr. John done and to help you grieve Miss Lucenia's passin', all them forestry circulars we went over, all the learnin' you give me about takin' care of my land. You got a lot of grit. Takin' on this business, I know you're feelin' shaky, but you're gonna do jest fine."

Annaliese grabbed him for a hug.

"Listen," Wade said as soon as he could look her in the eye again. "There's a grade of lumber that's shot full of holes from weevils and worms, but it still makes good boards, good and sound."

Annaliese smiled. "I know. It's called sound wormy."

"Yes, ma'am. That's it. Well, I reckon you're feelin' wormy right now."

She laughed, but her eyes brimmed with tears.

"But you're sound, Miss Annaliese."

And before she could grab him again, Wade went out the door.

After a few minutes of dabbing at her eyes, Annaliese dipped her new pen in the new inkwell.

May 11, 1903

Dr. Carl A. Schenck
The Biltmore Forest School
Asheville, North Carolina

Dear Dr. Schenck:

Allow me to introduce myself as the owner of a lumber company in north Georgia. I have read reports of your application of European scientific principles of forestry in America, specifically in Mr. George Vanderbilt's woodlands at his Biltmore estate, and of your establishment of a school for training young men in such. I would like to hire one of your graduates to work with me here in Georgia. Please reply as soon as possible to let me know if you will be able to send someone. This individual must be of the highest moral character, as there are many women and children on the property. I would appreciate receiving a background report on this candidate and your advice on appropriate renumeration.

Cordially,

A. Stregal
Owner, Stregal Brothers Lumber Company
P. O. Box 25
Pinch, Georgia

She addressed the letter and looked at it, this ticket to turmoil. Onto an already enflamed industry in the hottest timber market in the nation, she was pouring kerosene. This apprentice was going to be as welcome among her colleagues as a forest fire, not that they'd exactly be welcoming her either. The weight of the letter grew in her hands until it was so heavy she had to put it in the mailbag. She told herself the envelope was irretrievable, gone, already on the train to North Carolina. Back inside, she opened the top drawer of a filing cabinet and pulled the first file.

23

On Friday, as the blue fingers of last light inched across the sawmill compound, Henry and Hoyt rode in. The mill yard dogs trotted out, tails wagging at familiar faces and familiar men, and escorted them up the hill. Annaliese came out the door to wave, glass of bourbon in her other hand. Within minutes of walking into the house, Henry saw that the three women—no Olive in sight—were as taut as piano wire. While Phillip poured him a drink, he told Henry that the woman had up and quit for no good reason. Odd, he said, that she would've left wages and board, but the women were pretty tight-lipped about it, he said, and he'd learned long ago not to lift lids on domestic pots. Tight-lipped and frantic to get milk out of Ruth and Annaliese and into Georgia Ann, he added.

After supper, Henry lit a fire in the parlor while Annaliese settled into the rocking chair with the cranky newborn in her arms. Hoyt chose the settee opposite her. Henry sat off to the side, flexing five fingers against the other five.

While she tipped the cup to the baby's lips carefully, so carefully to make the thinnest of streams, Annaliese explained her plans for the land. Precious drops went down Georgia Anna's chin. Hoyt tried to pay attention to the boss, but his eyes kept going to the baby with its hideous mouth, the milk that dribbled out of the nose, the smacking and gulping.

He inched away in the slightest increments, which Annaliese did not miss.

Suddenly, Annaliese poured too much into the tiny mouth, and the baby erupted with gagging and spitting. Her panicked screams filled the room. Annaliese put the cup down and patted her back.

"So, you say we'll be clearing land for railroad tracks to be laid?" Hoyt shouted over the wailing.

"Yes, to get supplies in and the lumber out." Annaliese turned the baby around to look at her. Georgia Ann opened her eyes, took a deep breath. "We won't be driving timber down the rivers anymore," Annaliese said.

"And you say we'll be mapping all the land to decide how each parcel can best be used?"

"Some for commercial timbering, others for wildlife havens or watershed management." Annaliese brought the cup toward the baby again, but waited for her to stop wiggling.

"And you're still going to make money?" Hoyt tried to not sound incredulous.

"Yes, of course, Hoyt. I said we'll still be cutting trees," Annaliese said, trying the baby in her other arm, tilting the cup again.

Hoyt ran his hands over the thin strands of hair cupping his ears. "I thought I was jest goin' to get the crews back in the woods to keep trespassers out."

About five drops went down. Annaliese leaned in to see if they would be coming back out.

Henry sent Hoyt looks of warning, but Hoyt's horrified eyes were locked on the baby. He ran his hands up and down his legs. "But . . . well, you reckon them stumpers are going to take to all of this? To me? I was jest Mr. John's timber cruiser before."

Annaliese's head snapped up. "Stop rubbing your legs."

Hoyt's hands froze mid-thigh.

"They'll take to what I pay them to take to," Annaliese said. The baby let out a startled cry. Annaliese stuck her pinky in her daughter's mouth. "What do they care what they're doing as long as I pay them?" She started rocking.

Hoyt blinked, looked over at Henry, who was shaking his head no, not me, don't look at me. Look at her. The boss.

"Hoyt!" Annaliese whispered with heat. "Look at me." The man turned his face back to her. "You're the man to do this, Hoyt. I need you. You're honest and loyal, you know the land. You love it as much as I do."

Hoyt gave a stiff nod.

"Then help me save it."

Another nod.

Annaliese's rocking picked up. "People out there," she tilted her head to the hills beyond the fireplace, "are testing me. I won't have it."

"No, ma'am. I mean, yes, ma'am."

"Then you're with me?"

"Yes, ma'am."

"All right. We'll saddle up at eight o'clock tomorrow. I want to check on the seedlings I planted on Black Face Mountain."

Hoyt shot to his feet, extended his hand for a shake, saw her withering look that said that weren't her hands were occupied? He dropped it to his side where it hung like a ham on a string. With a hoarse goodnight, he left for his bunk in the stable.

Henry moved to the settee, still warm. "A little hard on him, weren't you?"

"How could he say 'You reckon them stumpers are going to take to this?' to me?" Anger flared in her eyes.

"It's a fair question, Anna."

Annaliese turned her attention to the squirming baby who had reached her limit with her mother's pinky.

"You're going to have to learn to separate family and business," Henry said, touching her arm.

Annaliese propped the baby up again, and while the fire crackled softly, she and the cup and the baby got into a better rhythm. After a while, the cup was empty. The baby's eyelids closed. Slowly, Annaliese pulled one hand away from the child to press her apology into Henry's hand. Her face softened as he pressed back.

Henry rested his forearms on his knees. A log on the fire crashed into the throbbing embers. In their glow, he could see the tears shining in her eyes. "What happened with Olive?" he asked.

She told him.

"And you believed her?" Shock rose in his voice and across his face.

"I think it's possible."

"What! Based on what evidence?"

"You sound like a lawyer."

"Based on what, Anna? I knew the man."

"Apparently not."

Henry looked at her.

"Olive knew things. About his body. His privates."

Henry sat back, stunned again. Annaliese was breaking rules every day, but what had just come out of her mouth broke astonishing new ground between them. Given that the restraints were now off, he thought about saying what was actually on his mind, which was that unless John had only one testicle or a spectacular birthmark or a spectacular penis (one way or the other), Olive could've said anything and been correct. After all, the distinctions in that region were measured quite subjectively. He felt confident that Annaliese wouldn't know a distinction there when she saw it, but he wasn't about to get into that.

Annaliese read the skepticism on his face. "And other things about him. Words he used to shout out." She looked at the floor. "During the moment of ecstasy."

Henry reeled again, but plunged on. "And Olive knew those words?"

"Yes. Two words."

Now Henry had to think very carefully before responding. Here was a much wider spectrum of possibilities. Given the miles on Olive, given that she knew John was urban and Catholic and educated, could she have made some good guesses at what he might bellow? Or did she actually bed him? Could John Stregal actually have been unfaithful? Henry thought he knew the man, but Henry had been fooled before by men whose public character was sterling, only to find out later the sterling was mere plating over mottled copper. Hadn't he wondered about John that one time for the way he looked at Ruth when she left the room? That ember of suspicion had died long ago.

"What two words?" Henry rubbed his hands over his rough knuckles, waiting to hear the usual.

"Two Latin words. Mater Dei."

Bewilderment spread across Henry's face. "What does that mean?"

"Mother of God," she said.

"Oh." There was nothing usual about that. "That's unique."

Finally, Annaliese thought. You see?

"I'm so sorry, Anna."

"Don't be. Now that I've had time to think about it, he did us a favor."

Henry looked at her sharply.

"He was so damned self-righteous with his blaming us for betraying him when we hadn't."

Henry had never heard her swear before either. He held his palms up to slow her down.

"One kiss in your office," she said. "One single kiss. No one saw us, but he must've seen something else between us somewhere and figured out how we felt about each other." As she got louder, the baby's eyes opened and closed.

"Sssshhh. Anna, all right, he saw our growing affection, but he knew we wouldn't act on it. He knew you're not the kind of woman who'd get in another man's bed," Henry whispered.

"Well, whatever he thought, he was out to punish us. He lured us to that mill that day, didn't he, to make sure we saw him get on that log heading into the saw." Her voice broke.

"Anna, stop." He reached for her hand. "Please try to remember him as the man who loved you and the children, who built this company so his family would be secure. That's the only reason he brought y'all to Georgia, and I'm so glad he did."

Annaliese rocked in her chair.

"Let's get out of here tomorrow, go for a ride." Henry said. "I've got something I want to show you."

"Henry, I can't leave. I just got here and I've got to find a wet nurse and—"

"Yes, you can. You can leave for a couple of hours. Ruth can feed the baby and put the word out for a wet nurse. Just a few hours."

Annaliese shrugged. "All right. But only if it's the day after tomorrow."

24

Dawson watched the riding party through his binoculars—the widow woman, her foreman, her boy, and the lawyer. He'd found that the lips in Pinch were remarkably loose when it came to Annaliese Stregal. People were happy, eager even, to share information about her, especially that grisly business about her husband and his brother. Jumped on a log heading into a saw, they said, the both of them. One a lunatic, the other all tore up over losing his wife in a riding accident. Mrs. Stregal owns it all, now, they said. She is Stregal Brothers Lumber Company.

That woman should be tending to her children, Dawson thought.

Riding four abreast and in no particular hurry, the riders crossed a pasture that led to Black Face Mountain, where Dawson's oxen and crews were cutting through her pine seedlings. The young pines, only as big around as a child's arm and flimsy as corn stalks, were going down like weeds at that moment. Dawson tucked the binoculars into his shirt and turned his horse toward the showdown with Annaliese Stregal.

A few minutes later, he emerged from the trees that lined the edge of her seedlings. Pickens, the foreman of the crew, saw him and motioned to the drag skinners to stop the oxen. Everything groaned—animals, wagons, men—as they rolled to a halt. After exchanging words with Dawson,

Pickens waved to the drag skinners to roll the wagons again. Dawson slipped back into the woods.

It was the boy who arrived first, on a horse that had raced ahead of the others. Dawson could clearly see the shock on his face. He turned the horse and kicked it back into the dust they had just stirred up. Dawson pulled a cloth sack labeled Indian Cigars and Cigarettes from a pocket. The image of the manufacturer's idea of an American Indian, with full white feather headdress and golden arrows crossed behind him, flattened out as Dawson pulled the drawstrings apart to pinch up a wad of tobacco. He rolled a cigarette, lit it, patted the horse's neck. "Won't be long now," he said. A few minutes later, the four riders galloped up to the mess—deep wagon tracks through the red mud, seedlings broken and flattened, and the backsides of men and beasts walking away from it all.

Annaliese jumped off her horse, pulled out a rifle, and shot it into the air. The sawyers turned around. She fired again. Pickens simply raised his hand to shield his eyes as he looked at her as if she were a lost cow.

Dawson came out of the woods on foot, waving his hat at her. "Hold on, hold there," he said.

"Those your men?" Annaliese asked.

"Who's asking?" Dawson's granite-hard look shifted from her to the man beside her.

Annaliese stalked over to get in front of his face. "I'm Annaliese Stregal and this is my land. You're trespassing."

"Henry Chastain," Henry said. "And you're vandalizing."

Dawson looked over at the trampled trees as if he'd never seen them before, raised his hands in defense. "I just rode in from North Carolina," he said. He called to the foreman who was watching from his end of the field. "Pickens! Get over here," he shouted. Then to Annaliese he said, "Dumbest bull of the woods in north Georgia." Back to Pickens—"Your shoes got as much mud in 'em as your head?"

"We're warning you, he's a lawyer," Samuel said. He jabbed a thumb in Henry's direction.

"Hold on, boy, just hold on," Dawson said, flipping his hat back onto his head. The tobacco sack fell out of his pocket. Everyone watched him get off the horse and pick it up.

"What's your name?" Annaliese asked.

"Dawson. Buck Dawson, ma'am."

"You stopped by my office a while ago. Spoke to my worker there about buying my land."

"Yes, ma'am," he said. Dawson looked at Pickens as though he couldn't wait to get his hands around his throat. "Can't you tell where them property lines are? You lose your compass?" he yelled.

Pickens glared back as he arrived in front of the boss. He ran a finger under his blade-like nose. Henry, Annaliese, Hoyt, and Samuel watched the exchange in stony silence.

Dawson jerked his head toward Annaliese. "This here is her land," he said.

"Sorry," Pickens said. His eyes were venomously red.

"I'm just all tore up about this. Sure am. I'll pay for the damages, Mrs. Stregal," Dawson said. His lips parted in a smile that revealed crooked, tobacco-stained teeth.

Annaliese shook her head. "I don't want your money. I want you to replant these trees," she said.

Dawson's cocky smile wilted. "Well, ma'am, that ain't what we do. Now if you'll jest let me settle up."

Annaliese walked over to a downed seedling, pulled it up, and shook its limp branches open. "This one. It could be all right. Trunk isn't broken." Her boot tamped the exposed roots back into their hole. "See? Like this." She wiggled the trunk in, tamped again.

Dawson's mouth twitched as he stared at her boot.

"As for the dead ones, you need to replace them. I'll show you how you can order more from the government," she said.

"The government." He tilted his head away to hide his disgust. "Well?"

He looked up at her.

Annaliese walked over to him with her rifle across an arm. "Take off your hat."

Despite his efforts, Dawson's lip curled with anger, but he managed to slowly remove his hat. His bald head, pale and liver-spotted, was as smooth as a knob of marble. She looked into his black, watery eyes, saw the muscles from temples to jaws working hard beneath the thick, colorless skin. The eyes were dead, like the thinnest of paper walls behind which there was no illumination. Cigarette stench came off his clothes.

She backed up and said, "My foreman here," she tilted her head toward Hoyt, "he'll stay to make sure this gets done right."

Hoyt snuck a look at Pickens, scowling and picking at the whitish scar that ran from one ear to his Adam's apple.

Dawson put the hat back on and shook himself back into the friendly-like pose he'd started with. "All right," he said. He waved at Pickens to get the men turned back. "Sure am sorry about this, Mrs. Stregal. It won't happen again. We'll be out of this county shortly." He smiled at her. "Unless you'd like to sell me some of your parcels."

"Nothing's for sale," Annaliese said.

Dawson watched her tuck her rifle behind her saddle and swing her trousered leg over the saddle, two things he'd never seen a woman of her standing do. As she rode away, he realized that he was going to have to think harder about how to bend Annaliese Stregal to his way of thinking.

25

Annaliese gave Dawson two days before she returned to make sure he'd done it right.

"Looks like they got them back in the ground pretty good," Henry said as they rode up to the field.

Annaliese got off her horse. "Not bad, I guess," she said, tapping the earth around a seedling after straightening it. They looked over the acres of rough land that Dawson's crews had repaired slapdash. "They'll settle in with the next good rain," Annaliese said.

"Yep. Pines are tough. Like you."

Annaliese laughed. "Dawson didn't like me one bit, did he? Uppity woman telling him what to do."

"Meanwhile," Henry said with a tilt of his head toward the road, "shall we continue, Mrs. Stregal?"

"Lead the way, Mr. Chastain."

They guided the horses to a sweep of land choked with locust and mountain laurel. Eventually, it opened into pasture of bushes, sassafras, and withered corn stalks. A massive chestnut tree stretched out its limbs luxuriantly over the field. A broken rail in the fence that had once defined the contours of the farming family's life let them into the old plow ground. A rude cabin and barn of bleached wood sagged inward. Annaliese imagined the ghost of the cow that had once turned toward the barn at the milking hour and the ghost of an aproned woman standing in the cabin's doorway looking at the backs of sons who had already hightailed it to the textile mills. But still the very real honeysuckle flowered along the rails of the tumbledown fence and narcissus had dutifully returned to cluster around the porch.

"Over there, when I was a boy," Henry said, pointing to a stand of low, wide trees along the fence, "wild pigeons roosted at night, hundreds of them. At dusk, they'd glide toward the trees like giant, gray cinders floating down. But one bitter cold night, a bunch of drunks came with torches and big sticks, slaughtered the birds. Seven hundred in one night."

Annaliese shook her head.

"For fun."

"Awful," she said.

They passed a rusted plow on its side, laced over with vines. "There were so many birds, the branches sank down to here." Henry's hand reached out to indicate shoulder-high.

"Why didn't they fly away?"

"Couldn't. They were freezing, exhausted."

Annaliese shook her head. "So many ways to harm what God gives us."

"They're gone now. Extinct." Henry's horse stopped to nibble on a thistle. "We Americans have always thought that nature will always provide. But some ancient cultures knew better. They saw trees as sacred," he said. "They believed that tree spirits helped humans by bringing rain, sun, and fertility. In Greece, Rome, and India, thousands of acres of trees were preserved for religious reverence."

Annaliese looked over at him in surprise.

"I read that in Sir James George Frazer's *The Golden Bough*."

"Well, Mr. Chastain," Annaliese said with new regard in her voice.

Henry chuckled softly.

"So, these trees, that story—is this why you brought me here?"

"Nope. Come on." Henry kicked his horse into a trot, then a gallop across the pasture. On his heels came Annaliese's horse, ears flattened, hooves pounding a steady drumming in the soft earth. The horses turned onto a skid road with a steeper grade that forced them to slow down. Beside the road, a crystal stream trickled over rocks carpeted with velvety mosses.

"Is it a waterfall? It's a waterfall you're taking me to, isn't it?" Annaliese asked, trying to catch her breath.

Henry got off and led the horses through the trees until the gray light of a clearing shone through.

The foundation of his cabin, twelve inches high now, was surrounded by red mud that had split into gelatinous chunks like a custard gone wrong. A turkey shot out from the cabin's center in startled retreat.

"Henry," Annaliese said. "This is yours? You're building this?"

"With my father, yes." Henry ushered Annaliese to a stump. He rolled another stump over and sat beside her, excited and goofy in the shoulders.

"Your father? I didn't realize he lived so close."

"Couple of miles away."

"I'd like to meet him."

"In time," Henry said with a laugh. "Don't want to run you off too soon. So, what do you think?" His hand swept across the foundation in front of them.

"I had no idea you knew how to do this."

"Thought maybe I might could bring Sam up here some time. Show him what I've learned."

She reached for his hand and turned it palm up. "So this is where these cuts and callouses came from." His cuffs were rolled back, revealing sun-browned skin and swirls of black hair.

"Like you, I'm building a foundation, Anna, for the rest of my life," he said.

He leaned in, kissed her hard, knocking her hat off. She kissed him back just as hard. They struggled to stand, still kissing, to press knees, hips, and chests together. Henry put a hand on her back and the other on her hair. Finally, he let her go. They looked at each other, surprised. Smiles broke out, then soft laughter. She took his face in her hands, and as she held him in that way of those who cherish, he kissed her again.

He led her to the hewn timbers, showed her how he and his father had slabbed off the sleepers inch by inch until the four sides were straight, pointed out the lap joints he'd carved, explained where the fireplace would be. "One day," he said, turning her around until she faced the mountains, "we'll sit on the porch and look at this."

The view from nearly five thousand feet above the valley floor took the eye clear to Tennessee. Three ranges of the ancient, calm mountains rose into the sky, each range higher than the one before, each flank more heavily veiled in vapor. Clouds followed one another in a steady march across the restless sky.

"In the morning, the mist hangs in those valleys so heavy the mountains seem to be rising out of a lake," Henry said.

"The breathing mountains," Annaliese said.

He kissed her neck. "I want to show you that, Anna. One morning."

She blinked into the light, grateful that he couldn't see her astonished face.

He turned her around again and pointed to a spot in the center of one of the long edges of the frame. "Here's where the steps will be. On that morning, we'll go back inside and I'll do this." He kissed her again, and this time his hand slid from her back to her waist. While she felt him grow hard against her, she wondered about Henry's body. Under all of those clothes, what did it look like, or, more specifically, under those pants. She'd only seen one pair of testicles in her life and assumed they all looked the same, but now she'd heard otherwise.

And just like that, she had invited John and Olive into the moment.

Henry felt the tension sweep through her. "What?" he asked.

"Nothing." She attempted a smile.

"You're not married any more, Anna. We're not doing anything wrong."

"I know."

He let go a little. "Do you love me?"

"It's not that, it's just that this is a little sudden, not that I don't enjoy—"

Henry, sensing an annoying comment about how much she enjoyed the pleasure of his company, backed away. "Do you love me or not, Annaliese? I'd like to hear you say it."

She looked at his earnest face, his nakedly honest face. He had such an upright heart. "Please give me some time. I want to be sure when I say what you're wanting to hear."

He tilted his head as he judged the veracity of that, but the shy wind that had been at their backs all day was gathering energy, and the trees were rustling, so he simply said, "Rain's coming. We'd better get on home."

26

Annaliese looked up from *American Lumberman Magazine* at the knock on the office door. Before she said a word, a young man opened it and headed straight for her. "Caleb Boone, ma'am," he said. "From the Biltmore School of Forestry." A smile creased his broad, sunburned face.

She shot up to grab his hand and pump it. "Yes, yes, Mr. Boone, welcome. Dr. Schenck wrote and said you were—"

Trying to withdraw his hand from the only female handshake he had ever encountered but doing so slowly so as not to offend, Caleb said, "Yes, ma'am, well, I'm looking for Mr. Stregal? Mr. A. Stregal?"

"Oh, that's me. Herschel could've met your train if I'd known when you were arriving."

He shook his head. Confusion gathered in his eyes. "You're A. Stregal?"

"Yes. Annaliese Stregal."

Caleb Boone grabbed his left elbow as if to lock himself down. His stony face held the expression of someone who had just peered into an open coffin. She waited, fingertips resting on her desk, trying to decide what to make of this candid response and the man himself. Would he be willing to take orders from a woman? He was short and wide, built like Wade, she thought, and with Wade's coffee-colored skin too, but milkier, and high cheekbones, not as chiseled. She guessed he was part Cherokee.

"Is there a brother?" He gestured to the outside, which she took to mean the sign that blazed Stregal Brothers Lumber Company across the sawmill.

"No, just me. Sole owner. The boss. All you've got." She was beginning to have her doubts.

He heard the edge in her voice. "Sorry, ma'am. I don't mean nothin' with all of these questions."

"Of course." Please stop, she thought. I want so badly for you to work out you have no idea.

"I'm just trying to understand."

"My husband and his brother began the business. They passed. It's mine now."

Caleb released his arm and nodded. "And you're wanting to do things different."

"Yes, that's why you're here."

His shoulders relaxed, and he scanned the room, as if to size her up based on the looks of the place.

"I have big plans, Mr. Boone, and the capital to realize them." Or at least try them, she thought.

He nodded slightly. "Yes, ma'am."

She could see in his eyes that more questions were brewing, but he said nothing.

"Please sit down," she finally said, waiting to see if he'd sit before she did.

He gestured for her to sit, then he lowered himself into the chair facing her desk, put his hat on his knee, and swatted at his hair to smooth it down. His teeth were as white as sanctuary marble and impossibly straight. His lumberman's mask of sunburned cheeks and pale forehead on a beardless face had not weathered more than twenty-five years, she figured. She knew little about him other than Dr. Schenck's testimony to his character. Dr. Shenck had suggested a salary of twenty dollars a month.

"So, where do you hail from, Mr. Boone?"

"Graham County, North Carolina, ma'am, born and raised."

"Lots of logging going on there."

"Oh, yes, ma'am. My pappy owns a sawmill there. Been in the woods all my life. I've always worked from cain't to cain't."

"Pardon?"

He threw his head back and laughed. "From cain't see before sunrise to cain't see after sunset."

"Well, we won't work you that hard," she said with a smile. "So you've just graduated from the forestry school?"

He nodded. "Spent a year there. I've seen terrible things with logging. So many of our grandfather trees coming down, it just tears me up. I heard about Dr. Schenck. Went there to see what the fuss was all about."

"I'm anxious to see what you can teach me."

"Yes, ma'am," he said, scooting forward as though ready to pull a wagonload of logs himself at that very moment.

She came around the desk. "Let's get you settled. I'll show you where you'll bunk. Supper's at six-thirty."

At six-twenty-five, he came to the kitchen door and Ruth let him in. Samuel and Emeline ran in from the hall to stare at his wet-combed black hair and the cowboy boots with tooled scrolls and silver tips. His head bobbed as he ticked off children—one, two, plus a baby in a high chair stuffing sweet potatoes in her nose.

"Now that 'un is mine," Ruth laughed. "Lucy. Pert near six months old."

Annaliese swept in with Georgia Ann, who grinned her heartbreaking grin at the stranger. Both women braced for Caleb's reaction.

"Hey there," Caleb said with no reaction at all as he reached for the baby's hand. "What's your name? I bet you run the place. How old?" He wiggled her index finger.

Annaliese's shoulders relaxed. "Six weeks. This is Georgia Ann."

He shook the finger. "Pleased to meet you, Miss Georgia Ann."

Ruth wiped an eye with the back of her hand.

The children tugged on Annaliese to be introduced. Stooping to shake each sticky little hand, Caleb nodded with serious acknowledgement of the pleasure of meeting them. His smooth face glowed like a welcoming hearth.

Samuel stepped on Caleb's boot toe. "I can shoot a rifle good," he said.

"Well. You shoot a rifle well, Sam," Annaliese said.

"That right?" Caleb asked.

Ruth said, "Sure enough he does. I find a bag of rabbits or doves in this here sink 'bout once a week."

"Mama shot a mountain panther flat dead last year," Samuel said with rising excitement.

"It was after me in the chicken coop," Emeline yelled over her brother.

Caleb looked at Annaliese and she nodded.

"Take me with you when you and Hoyt go timber cruising?" Samuel asked.

Annaliese put her hand on her son's shoulder. "We'll see. You'll have school starting back up in July."

"I'm old enough, Mama. I'm almost nine years old," Samuel said with a dip of the shoulder to escape her. "Don't you think, Mr. Boone?"

Caleb recognized the snare of apron strings in front of him. "Right tall for eight, ain't ya?" he finally thought to say.

"Almost, nine," Samuel said.

A covered dish pushed open the back door, followed by Dorothy, followed by a pie in Phillip's hands, followed by a young woman who lived in the hills behind the home. Winnie came three times a day to feed Georgia Ann and leave milk in the icebox. She took Georgia Ann from Annaliese, fetched a cup from a cabinet, and went to the back porch. After more introductions, the family flowed into the dining room, where Samuel lit the sconces and candles. Dorothy slid a pillow onto a chair for Emeline and helped her up.

After grace was said and the dishes of food started around, Emeline looked up at Caleb beside her and said, "Are you an Indian?"

"Partly," Caleb said.

"Mr. Wade is an Indian," Emeline said. "He cut up our hog last year. His name was Deuteronomy."

Dorothy looked at the ham on her plate, pointed her fork at it, and shot a questioning glance at her sister, who shrugged that she had no idea whether Deuteronomy was on the menu tonight or not.

"Mr. Wade tells us Cherokee stories," Emeline said.

"Like the one about Long Man," Samuel said.

"Yep. Long Man's the spirit living in the river with his head in the mountains and his toes in the sea," Caleb said.

Emeline tilted her head at Caleb. "What? He never told us that."

"And the one about how the insects make music with their legs," Samuel said.

"Did he tell you about the Nunnehi?" Caleb asked. "The Little People?"

"No! Tell us," Samuel said.

"Hold on." Caleb got up and crept to the window, scanned the sky, and came back.

"What are you doing?" Samuel asked.

"Wanted to make sure the sun hasn't set yet. You shouldn't talk about them after nightfall," Caleb whispered.

The adults exchanged amused glances. Sunlight would be bathing the mountains for at least another hour.

"Or what?" Samuel asked.

"You just shouldn't is all," Caleb said.

"Tell us," Emeline said.

"The Nunnehi can't be seen by man unless they allow it. When they do, they look like any other Cherokee except they're very small and have long hair, hair so long it reaches the ground."

"Are they bad?" Emeline asked.

"Well, they're mischievous, but they often help children who are lost in the woods. That's where they live, in mountain caves or mountain laurel thickets. Sometimes, though, they build a house under the mountain. On a small branch of the Cheoah River near my home in North Carolina, there's a hole in the ground. A warm cloud comes out of it. People say the Nunnehi have a house down there and they've built a fire. In the winter, hunters go there to warm themselves but they won't stay long."

"Why not?" Emeline asked.

"The Little People don't like being disturbed. If someone bothers them too many times, that person will be puzzled, touched in the head for the rest of his life."

"But not children. They like children," Emeline said. "Don't they?"

"Depends."

Dorothy shot Annaliese a look to stop him, but Annaliese waved her to over to the sideboard. As Annaliese sliced into the pie, she whispered, "Let's see how he handles this." "I hope he's got good sense with children," Dorothy said. "We're about to find out," Annaliese said.

Caleb began. "A boy about ten was playing at the river one day. A man came along and said, 'Come with me to my house and rest a while.' The boy said no, that he was going home to eat soon. The man said, 'I'll give you supper, let you spend the night, and take you home in the morning.'"

"I'd never do that," Samuel said with a quick glance at his mother.

"'Course not," Caleb said. "But the boy went with him and had a nice dinner and played with his children. In the morning, the man took him down a path that had been there for many years, a path first made by deer, then the wolves that tracked them, then the Cherokee, who planted peach trees along one side and corn on the other." He nodded thanks as Dorothy put a plate of pie in front of him.

"I've seen those wild peach trees," Samuel said.

"Sam, it's just a story," Emeline said with a roll of her eyes.

"They came to another trail, and the man told the boy to follow it back to the river where they'd met. The man left him, and when the boy got back to the river, he found a crowd of people searching the water and bank. When they saw him they ran toward him shouting, 'Here he is. He's alive!'"

Annaliese placed the plate of pie in front of Emeline, who pulled it closer, with her eyes on Caleb.

"His mother hugged him and asked where he'd been. The boy explained everything, pointing toward the peach trees and cornfields they'd passed. The mother said, 'There are no peach trees and no cornfields up there. There is no house. But we hear a drum up there sometimes. You were with the Nunnehi.'"

"And they were nice to him," Emeline said as she curved a spoon through her pie.

"Yes, but the mother warned that when the Little People choose to show themselves, it is not to be spoken of for seven years afterward." Caleb picked up a fork and sank it into the pie.

Samuel looked at his mother and aunt for his pie, which was being pushed across the table to him. "And they're still out there?" he asked.

"Well, I'm only half Cherokee, Samuel," Caleb said. "So I reckon I only hold to this 'bout halfways."

A breeze swept in like a gust of rain, flattening the candle flames left and right until they finally died. The children paid no attention, but the adults sat up straighter in their chairs.

The sound of the sawmill dogs broke the silence. Two dogs, then three, getting all worked up. The dining room emptied onto the porch where everyone strained to see who would be traveling at this hour in these mountains. A slumped figure came slowly toward them on a horse too tired to kick at the dogs. Phillip stood beside Annaliese at the lip of the porch. Herschel came around the house, rifle in hand. The rider dismounted with the weight of many miles on his shoulders and led his horse toward the family.

"Mrs. Stregal," he called out. The accent was not a local one.

"Who's there?" Phillip asked, going down one step.

"They said in town I'd find Mrs. Stregal up here," the man said as he removed his hat. He finally came close enough for them to see the fine cut of his black coat, his young and clean-shaven face, the clerical collar.

Annaliese stepped forward. "Yes?" she asked.

"I'm Father Thurmond from the diocese office. Down in Savannah? You sent for a priest?"

"Oh, my goodness!" Annaliese rushed down the steps. "My goodness, you're here! So quickly."

"By the grace of God and that poor horse," Father Thurmond said with a smile. His unlined, boyish face held an expression of gratitude and eternal optimism. "I hear you've got a baby needs baptizing?"

27

After breakfast, Ruth smoothed a tablecloth edged in Venetian lace across the dining room table and placed in its center the bowl she loved most, a mint-green Chinese bowl wrapped in white cranes and pink lotus flowers in high relief. She emptied a pitcher of water into it. The family filtered into the room in their starched whites with much pulling and scratching at collars. Herschel arrived with Lucy in his arms, ablaze in a red dress and red bonnet, followed by the priest, white surplice draped around his shoulders, and Dorothy, Phillip, Annaliese, and Georgia Ann wearing a white batiste dress that swallowed her. The priest stared at the baby's mouth without a word, but he reached out to cup her head, suddenly grasping the urgency of her mother's summons weeks ago, not that he could've reached her in time had things gone badly.

Annaliese watched the priest's face. "We've gotten her to six weeks," she whispered, as if to protect the baby from learning of her vulnerability. "Eight and a half pounds on the scale this morning. So far, so good."

Father Thurmond cleared his throat. "We are gathered for this joyous occasion of bestowing Christian life on this little one," the priest said. He patted Georgia Anna's head. "Mrs. Stregal, you have asked to have your child baptized. In doing so you are accepting the responsibility of training her in the practice of the faith. Do you clearly understand what you are undertaking?"

"I do."

Father Thurmond turned to Dorothy and Phillip. "As this child's godparents, are you willing to support her religious upbringing and assume all responsibility for her if necessary?"

"We are," Phillip said, taking Dorothy's hand.

"What name do you give your child?" the priest asked.

"Georgia Ann Stregal," Annaliese said.

He blinked. "But you're supposed to name a child in honor of a saint."

Dorothy leaned in. "Ann is a saint," she said.

"But Georgia," the priest said. "I don't know. I might need to ask the bishop about this."

"You're fresh out of the seminary, aren't you?" Phillip asked.

"Last month," the priest said defensively.

"Well, you're going to have to make decisions on your own in these hills, Father Thurmond," Annaliese said.

"I could get in trouble," the priest answered.

"We won't tell," Annaliese said.

"There's a Saint George, right?" Dorothy said. "George, Georgia, what's one more syllable?"

Father Thurmond pondered these suddenly mutinous people. Emeline walked on top of his shoes to get to her mother. The baby grunted with the effort of passing something.

"It's all right, Father," Annaliese said.

"Very well." The priest threw his shoulders back to try to re-establish authority. "And what do you ask of God's Church for Georgia Ann?"

"Eternal life," Annaliese said.

The priest began murmuring Latin prayers as he traced the sign of the cross on the baby's forehead, sending her into confused baby blinking. Ruth stood behind Emeline, patting her shoulders.

Having heard baptisms in Latin all of their lives, the Stregals understood what the priest was saying, that the prayers were about the mystery of death and resurrection and welcoming the new family member to the faith. They took comfort in the lyrical and ancient language, but the children did not. Emeline stood on tiptoe to run her fingers over the crane that flew across the green sky, almost pushing the bowl over but for Ruth's quick hand. Annaliese's mind wandered to future sacraments for Georgia Ann—First Communion, a Confirmation, and Holy Matrimony. With the same hope in her heart, Dorothy rested her hand on Annaliese's arm. When Father Thurmond began asking for blessings from a long list of the Church's most revered figures, the sisters recognized their cue to respond.

"Sancti Ioanness Baptistae," Father Thurmond was saying. *Saint John the Baptist.*

"Ora pro nobis," the adults said. *Pray for us.*

"What does that mean?" Samuel asked.

"It means pray for us," Dorothy whispered. "Hush."

Ruth clutched her Bible to her chest and cut her eyes over at Herschel, squinting at the babble.

"Sancti Ioseph," Father Thurmond said. *Saint Joseph.*

"Ora pro nobis," the adults said.

"Sanctorum Petri et Pauli." *Saints Peter and Paul.*

"Ora pro nobis."

"Sancta Maria, Mater Dei." *Holy Mary, Mother of God.*

"Ora pro nobis," Phillip said by himself. He opened his eyes and looked over at his wife, who was staring at the priest as if he'd said something offensive, as was Annaliese, as was Ruth.

"Omnes sancti et sanctae," Father Thurmond said into his book, finger pointing to his place. *All holy men and women.*

"Ora pro nobis," Phillip said again by himself.

The priest looked up and found three women staring at him. "Now what have I done?" he asked.

"Father, could we go back to English?" Annaliese asked.

The priest hesitated at this second violation of the rules, but clearly it was time to just wrap things up and get back on his horse. He raised his hands in the way he was taught, to implore God's benevolence. "My dear brothers and sisters, let us ask our Lord Jesus Christ to look lovingly on this child who is to be baptized, on her parents and godparents, and on all the baptized."

"Yes, Lord," Ruth whispered.

"Almighty and ever-living God, you sent your only Son into the world to cast out the power of Satan, spirit of evil, to rescue man from the kingdom of darkness—"

"Amen, Lord!" Ruth said.

"—and bring him into the splendor of your kingdom of light. We pray for this child. Set her free from original sin, make her a temple of your glory, and send your Holy Ghost to dwell with her."

"We ask this through Christ our Lord," the priest said.

"Amen," everyone else said.

The priest looked down for the little girl who had walked on his shoes. He tapped her shoulder and handed her a white bib with embroidered candle. Annaliese lowered the baby to Emeline and nodded to her to drape the bib across the baby's chest, then to Samuel to remove her white cap.

"Georgia Ann Stregal, this garment is a sign of your new life in Christ," the priest said, picking up a teacup, another deviation, but he plunged on. Annaliese moved the baby over the bowl. "And now I baptize you in the name of the Father, and the Son and the Holy Ghost," the priest said quickly as he poured water over the baby's head.

Afterward, Annaliese walked with Father Thurmond to the stable.

"You're sure you can't stay another night, Father? Give yourself a rest?" She looked over his face so young, so clueless about the dilemmas upon which the faithful were going to impale him for the next forty years.

"Mighty kind of you, Mrs. Stregal, but I've got a string of north Georgia towns to get to." The priest put his leather bag down to pull on his coat.

"Which ones?"

"Jasper, Tate, Canton for starters."

"Canton. There are Catholics in Canton?"

"Yes, ma'am. I've got another baptism there." Father Thurmond watched Herschel approaching with his horse. "Something I should know about Canton, Mrs. Stregal?"

"No, no, I'm just surprised to hear there are Catholics there. Do you suppose they speak Latin?"

"Latin," the priest repeated to hide his discomfort. Herschel handed him the reins, put his finger to his hat, and headed off to Ruth's list of the day. Father Thurmond tied his bag behind the saddle and got on the horse. As his freedom from this peculiar family was at hand, he felt free to blurt out, "Is there a problem around here with Latin?"

Shading her eyes more from his scrutiny than the sun, Annaliese said, "Just wondering if there's someone else out there like me, reluctant pioneer from the city, a Catholic adrift in a sea of Protestants."

Father Thurmond cocked his head at her. "Tell you what." He wiggled into his saddle and stirrups. "When I've finished my circuit, I'll let you know what I find out there."

"Safe travels, Father," Annaliese said. She watched his horse take him down the hill and disappear behind the sawmill. You won't find what I need out there, she thought. One man, one other man who would choose two specific Latin words to moan helplessly inches above the ears of Olive Washburn.

Back at the house, Ruth and Dorothy waited on the front porch. "We heard that," Ruth said.

Annaliese shrugged. "I just wanted to—"

"Ruth has an idea," Dorothy said, putting her hand on Ruth's back. "Go on, Ruth."

"I've got this cousin. She was born with a caul, meanin' she was born in a sack of water that never broke. So there's a notion that babies born like that have a gift for seein' the future, seein' the truth of things, too, like who kilt somebody, that sort of thing."

"Seeing the truth of things?" Annaliese asked.

"We need to call on her. Name's Truth. Now you know a person named Truth cain't tell no lies."

"Lies about what?"

Dorothy and Ruth looked at her. "You know," Dorothy said.

"Olive, you mean?"

"Olive and John," Dorothy said.

"She helped cousin Zero," Ruth said. "Born on the coldest night of 1850. Zero degrees," Ruth said.

"And what did Truth tell her?" Annaliese asked. "Or him."

"Truth said that Zero's mule that was missin' was over to the Wilkenses' corn field pert near twenty miles away."

Annaliese smiled at this claim. Twenty miles away over hill and dale in these mountains was impossibly far for a mule that would've been tracked by panthers and bears, but she wasn't surprised that the creative Scots-Irish, blatant boasters and robust storytellers all, might embellish the story in the telling and retelling.

"Sure enough, that's where the mule was," Ruth said.

Annaliese shook her head. "I want to put Olive behind me."

"Let's see what's Truth's got to say. Might could give you some peace," Ruth said.

"This sounds a little like, well, it has a whiff of—" She tried to find a word that wouldn't insult Ruth, who meant well, but Annaliese was thinking witchcraft. A Catholic had no business getting involved with witchcraft. She shook her head. "No, I don't think so."

"Miss Annaliese, Baptists don't want nothing to do with haints and witches neither, but she ain't no witch."

"Ruth, I know you mean to help." Annaliese brushed past the two women. "Who's watching the baby?"

28

Annaliese stopped at the sawmill doorway, took a deep breath, and headed straight for the bandsaw. Through the sleepless night before, images of its teeth circling on the ten-foot loop kept her awake. She'd made up her mind to seize the hideous thing, or rather, its control over her. As she approached the blades that gleamed under a fresh coat of gear oil, she forced herself to stare at them. She stood within inches of them and the empty carrier that had fed that log and her husband into them, stared at the floor where she had vomited and collapsed into his blood. Tomorrow, she'd face the saw and carrier and floor again, and the day after, and the day after that, until the new images had lost their power over her. With her heartbeat coursing in her neck, she forced herself to stand there. Sparrows swooped and chirped beneath the tin roof.

Caleb coughed in the doorway. She waved him in but didn't walk toward him until she trusted her legs.

Together they roamed the cavernous building lined with water buckets on one wall, inspected the conveyor belt with its spiked chains that hauled in the naked logs from the millpond. They passed a table of hammers, hooks, and filing tools lined up uniformly like surgical instruments. With all of this they took their time, for Caleb liked to announce the manufacturer and purpose of everything he touched. As they approached the millpond doors, they saw the sawyers standing at the water's edge. Backlit by the light bouncing off the pond, the men's faces were unreadable, but Annaliese could tell they were staring at her trousers.

"Morning," she said with a nod in their direction.

With mumbles, the men more or less responded.

She stepped forward to extend her hand to one of them. "Please tell me your name. I want to know each of you," she said.

Startled, the man looked left and right, then said, "Sullivan, ma'am. Amos Sullivan."

She looked him in the eye and moved to the next man. As each name was given, she repeated it, trying to isolate a nose or jaw or hair texture and link it to a word that she hoped would enable her to recall the name later. The group's attention was shifting, however, to the man beside her.

"Gentlemen, I'd like to introduce you to Caleb Boone. Brought him on board to teach us a few things," she said.

"Nice outfit you got here," Caleb said with a sweep of his hand behind him. "A gang edger in there. Electricity, too." He pointed toward the generator that stood beside the building. "Durn."

A thin man in overalls said, "Mr. Stregal, he ran this place right."

"I can see that. I grew up working in a sawmill," Caleb said.

Someone spit a stream of tobacco juice onto the silver tip of Caleb's tool scrolled boots. "Thought you was here to hug trees," the man said.

"Well, no, not—" Caleb said.

"You got some Cherokee in you?" someone else asked. "That coal black hair of yorn."

"How old are you?" yet another voice asked.

Caleb considered the gravel for a moment. "Y'all done a good job takin' care of the place," he said.

The sound of footsteps on gravel sent the men into straighter postures. Hoyt walked up, coffee mug in hand.

Annaliese put her hands in her pockets and said hello.

"Morning, ma'am," Hoyt said with a glance to judge whether she was in a better mood this morning.

A sawyer stepped forward to get in Hoyt's face. "So you're our bull of the woods now, huh?" The man jerked a thumb at Caleb. "And what about him? He goin' to tell us what we can't cut down?"

"How're we goin' to make a livin' here now?" said a short man with a pockmarked face that looked like rocky river bed.

"Now y'all hold on. We're still going to be cutting timber," Annaliese said. "With this new way, there will be jobs for all of you for years to come."

"And what would that way be?" someone asked.

"Selective cutting. Replanting and seeding. Making roads to get the timber out. No more using the rivers to drive it down here to the mill. No more dynamiting splash dams and ripping up the riverbanks, killing fish, killing people," Annaliese said. "Too much timber is lost that way, and depending on the rains makes us worse off than the farmers."

"Then how you goin' to get lumber to the mill?" the man in overalls asked.

"Locomotives," Annaliese said.

"Railroad? On these hills?" he asked.

Annaliese could see Caleb swaying beside her, itching to talk again, so she hurried to answer. "There's this new locomotive, the Shay narrow gauge. Small and built to climb hills."

The sawyers exchanged glances.

Caleb lost all restraint. "We're going to fight erosion on the slopes that have already been clear cut," he blurted. "At the bottoms of the gullies, we'll to drive in poles and weave branches in between. At the tops, we'll lay rough wickerwork in rows, short but thick."

These exclamations were met with squint-eyed looks.

Annaliese glanced at Hoyt's half-closed eyes that were avoiding hers. "Well, that's a talk for another day," she said.

"We gonna get paid the same?" the man with the pocked face said.

"Not what Mr. Stregal awarded you. Y'all know that was a mistake, but you'll receive a fair renumeration," Annaliese said.

"I cain't work for that," the man said with indignation.

"It means fifty cents a day," Annaliese said. "If you don't think that's fair, I know I can find twenty other men for every one of you who wants to argue."

The men went still.

She began talking faster. "As I was saying, selective cutting is cutting only those trees that will bring top dollar at that moment, like the yellow poplars right now."

"I heard that a Yankee company is buying 'em for tables," a man said.

"Right. Singer Sewing Company, for dozens of garment factories in northern cities," Annaliese said. "And we're going to process our timber byproducts, like oak tan-bark for tanning leather."

"You're goin' to cook tannic acid?" asked a man with a droopy mustache tipped with golden ambeer.

"And sell it to tanneries, yes," Annaliese said. "We'll capture the sawdust, too, and the woodchips, and wood pellets. There's a market for those."

"Huh," the man said.

"Listen," Caleb said, uncrossing his arms. "Y'all are going to learn things that will make you valuable workers. You're going to learn how to identify every species of tree, and all of the timber grades, and the values of those grades for the inspectors."

Hoyt looked down at the rocks as he kicked them the pond.

Caleb pumped his hands in the air. "Dr. Schenck taught us all of this. He insisted we learn what he called 'those hellish inspection rules', and do you know one day we had students from that new forestry school at Yale attending his lecture to learn this stuff, and they had no idea what he was talking about? Ha! Yale students didn't know!"

The crew, still as granite, squinted at him.

"Well, anyway," Annaliese said.

Caleb smoothed his hair. "Yes, anyway. You'll have jobs and good learning for years to come."

"When do we start?" someone asked.

Hoyt looked up.

"Tomorrow," Annaliese said. "We're going to cut a road to a big stand of oaks on Bloodroot Mountain. Today, check that the wagons are still sound, and load them with the whipsaws, skidders, poleaxes, chains, and everything else we'll need. Check the horses' shoes, make sure nobody's lame."

The men shuffled off. Caleb ran his fingers through his hair as he watched them fan out across the mill yard.

"How old *are* you, by the way?" Annaliese asked.

"Twenty-two."

Hoyt slapped his back. "Done missed your calling, son. I think there's a pulpit waiting somewhere for you."

"He's staying right here. Let's go," Annaliese said.

29

Samuel steered the wagon into Pinch's livery stable and jumped out to help his mother down. The tang of saddle leather and fresh hay washed over them as they followed the ringing of hammer on horseshoe to the aproned farrier. Seeing them approach, he straightened up from his anvil. They led him to their wagon, and Samuel described what the two horses needed. He pointed at the hooves, hands flying to indicate re-shoeing, filing, nailing, in short everything the farrier could see for himself, but he let the boy's exuberance play out.

In those gestures, Annaliese saw John. The boy, a month shy of nine, had his father's way of caressing every noun with fluid fingers, his way of nodding as he listened to imply that he agreed, which kept people talking while he was still deciding whether he in fact did. He had the same intense eye contact that made you think that what you were saying was the most fascinating thing he'd ever heard. But it was fear, not pride, that rose in her heart. What else besides charm was blooming in that pure, innocent brain even as John's tortured brain rotted in his grave, she wondered. For that matter, what dark behaviors were colonizing in all three of her children? When would the father's stain show itself? Hot temper, crazy spending, swearing, sleeping all day, stalking the moon all night—would those be the mere lurchings of adolescence or the permanent imprint of John? It would take years to know.

Which of the three might put the company at risk when they came of age, and which of them could stop that? Would it be Samuel holding it together while under attack from one sister headstrong and cynical or the other sister disfigured, withdrawn, angry at the world? Or would it be one of the girls, toughened by the indignities showered upon their gender, who would save the company from their brother?

Samuel's laugh—John's laugh—jolted her from her thoughts. She stepped outside.

Samuel strode out of the livery two inches taller and took his mother's elbow as if she needed to be guided around horse manure in the road and spittle on the boardwalk, and she let him. They joined Henry at Meddling's, full of people raising napkins hello as the three of them sat down in the dining room.

Thessalonia rushed over with a basket of biscuits. "Hey, Mrs. Stregal, Mr. Chastain, Sam. How y'all doin'?" She leaned over Annaliese to put the basket down.

"Fine, thank you, Miss Meddling," Annaliese said into the napkin she was unfolding. Thessalonia reeked of onions and bacon grease and a perfume of questionable provenance.

"Y'all hear that Milo Hawkins died? Lord, he was the devilishist man in the county," Thessalonia said.

"Now that's certainly saying something," Annaliese said. "But we musn't speak ill of the dead." She shot a meaningful look at her son.

"Bad to drink, that Milo. He always said he was goin' to raise enough hell to deserve to go there," Thessalonia said.

"And he did," Henry said with a grin. "But it's not for me to say where he ended up," he hurried to add.

"What's the special today?" Annaliese said.

"Fish. So, how's the baby doin'?" Thessalonia asked.

"She weighs nine pounds now," Samuel said as he took a biscuit.

Thessalonia turned back to Annaliese. "You aimin' to get her mouth fixed?"

The women at the table next to them stopped talking and began cutting up their food into infinitesimal pieces.

"She's fine," Annaliese said.

"Surgery. That's got to scare you," Thessalonia said.

Annaliese smoothed her napkin again.

"Well, when she starts tryin' to talk, I reckon you'll get around to that. How's that sawed-off forestry feller doin'? The one from North Carolina? The one they're callin' Stumpy?"

"His name is Caleb, Miss Meddling. He's doing well. What kind of fish and how is it prepared?" Annaliese asked.

"The usual way. How come that Olive woman run off? I told Corinthia she was trouble."

Forks and knives at other tables slowed.

"Y'all have some kind of fallin' out? Good thing you got another wet nurse. I heard Winnie come to help you with that." Thessalonia rubbed the knob at the top of Annaliese's chair.

Samuel looked up from his biscuit.

Annaliese put her hands on the table and nailed Thessalonia with a look sweeter than molasses. "Would you like to be introduced to Caleb, Miss Meddling? He's a bachelor, as I'm sure you've heard." She watched smiles bloom throughout the room. Recently, Annaliese had been, for once, on the receiving end of some town gossip. Ruth told her that Thessalonia scared off even Erastus Whitcomb, a one-armed widower with ten children. Thus, Thessalonia was back where she always was: On the hunt with all of the game downwind and fleeing.

For an instant, a gleam shone in Thessalonia's eyes, but she recovered with an arching of her back. "Mrs. Stregal! Such a personal question." She flipped her skirt as she spun away.

By two o'clock, Samuel was bending the farrier's ear again as he inspected his work. He drove the wagon to a spot alongside the boardwalk where his mother and Henry waited with a pile of packages. After all of the loading and goodbyes, their wagon pulled out of town.

Ten miles up the road, the wind rose, sending the trees swaying. Pinecones rained down and leaves skittered across the darkening road. The jittery mares flattened their ears as Samuel snapped the reins to get a head of steam for what was coming up—the covered bridge they hated. Chatty no more, the boy was focused on urging the girls through its shadows, the noise bouncing off the rafters, the sight of rushing water between the boards. Annaliese was watching him closely, trying to decide whether to take the reins. As they approached the bridge, though, she saw a man on a horse on the other side, standing sideways in the road, blocking them.

Buck Dawson didn't move as the boy pulled the horses to a stop. Just short of the bridge, they began the nervous dancing that he had hoped to avoid.

"Well, if it ain't Mrs. Stregal and her son coming from town," Dawson called out as he rode under the roof.

Annaliese inched her boot heel backward to confirm the rifle under the seat.

"Ma'am, I'd like to talk business with you for a minute," Dawson said. His voice and the horse's hooves echoed off the rafters.

"I'm not selling," Annaliese called out.

"Sure, sure." Dawson emerged into the gray light and stopped in front of the horses. He pulled his sack of tobacco and rolling papers out of a pocket. "Then how about selling me the timber rights to one or two of your parcels?" He calmly began rolling a cigarette. "I'll be in and out of your land before you know it."

"No, I don't think so," she said, making motions at him to get out of their way.

Dawson lit his cigarette. "I'll tell you straight out, Mrs. Stregal, that there's red oak, chestnut, and a small stand of poplars on one of your tracts. I'll give you a fair price, say, twenty-thousand dollars?" He took a drag on the butt, already filthy.

"No one's buying red oak right now," Annaliese said. "You don't want that oak. I know what you're after."

Samuel jerked the reins, but the horses kept banging into each other. Annaliese grabbed her shaky seat.

"All due respect, ma'am, I got to hurry to get that timber down. As a favor to you, we'll cut down any dead trees we find."

"Of course." She finally turned her body square to him. "Of course you're in a hurry."

"Ma'am?" Dawson cocked his head.

"In a hurry to get what you can before the federal government steps in. In a hurry to race across the land without thought or care, bloodying it and the rivers into death because of greed. Pure greed."

Dawson leveled a look at her. "Ain't greed. It's my callin'."

"No bird, no fish, no animal, not even the ants will be able to live within thirty miles of there when you're finished. Maybe I'll just leave those trees for all eternity, protected from lust like yours, so my children and their children will be able to see what the native people saw when they first stepped into these magical hills. Some of those poplars are probably four hundred years old. Surrender that land to you? Never."

Dawson's face darkened. "In that case, I hope nothin' happens to them trees. Fungus, tornado, fire."

"Get out of our way," Samuel yelled, as his wagon jerked left and right.

"Biggity damn woman," Dawson said. He leaned toward the wagon and flicked the red cigarette at Samuel.

Annaliese brushed the burning butt from his leg to the floor, and snatched up her rifle. While Dawson hightailed it for the woods, she took aim at a spot behind his horse's hooves and pulled the trigger. A explosion of dirt flew up exactly where she intended. The horse shied at the spray and stumbled. The last thing she saw as Samuel whipped the team forward was Dawson's horse going down and Dawson's shoulder heading toward an outcropping of granite.

30

The hiring call went out. Men came down from the hills to sign up at the sawmill office for their old jobs. Strangers came from distant states for the new railroad jobs—the laying of tracks, the tuning of engines. The commissary clerk returned to restock his shelves with tobacco, flour, coffee, salves, tonics, saddle soap, shoe sole leather, kerosene oil, lamp wicks, and boxes of peppermint sticks for Samuel and Emeline, his favorite customers. Hoyt found that with all of the timbering going on, teamsters and their trained oxen were scarce, but untrained oxen on steep mountainsides were out of the question. Animals that didn't know how to sidestep on command out of the skidway when a load of logs broke loose risked limb and life, including any human life that got dragged into the tangle. With Stregal dollars flowing freely, he raided the competition with glee, there being nothing more eternal in the Georgia mountains than grudges.

Wade and his brother, Tote, began building the tanbark distillery in a space between the sawmill and dry kiln. The pounding of their hammers joined the roar of the generator being tested, new railcars rolling in, and excited dogs.

By early June, the brothers had the one-story frame up, an airy outline the sawyers looked at skeptically every time they passed by. No one had bothered to collect bark before. Wade told his brother to never mind them. Just because the men never heard of such a thing didn't mean it was a bad idea, he'd said as they raised the oak beams into the brilliant sky. On the day that two wagons of distillery equipment pulled into the millyard, the brothers had begun framing the roof. Wade climbed down the ladder and waved the driver over.

"Need to unload these," the man said.

"You got the supply list?" Wade asked, raising his hand for it.

"What, you sayin' it ain't all here?" the man asked. He sent a scornful look back to his buddy driving the second wagon. Samuel appeared beside the first wagon, half-eaten apple in hand. Wade motioned again to be given the order sheet. The driver handed it to Samuel, who handed it to Wade.

"Two boilers," Wade said as he and Samuel walked around the crates to look for them.

"Yonder," the wagon driver said, pointing to the second wagon.

"Twenty hundred-gallon wooden vats and one copper vat, two hundred-sixty-four gallons."

"Back there, too," the driver said.

Wade had called out electric lights, motor, pumps, filters, and one wrought iron hot water tank when the driver said, "Look, I ain't got all day. It's all here. Cain't we just unload this so we can get back to town?"

"Almost done." Wade wrote something on the sheet.

"Give that here." The driver yanked the sheet from Wade's hands and walked him around the wagons to point out everything else, ending with a huge crate labeled sulphuric acid in large black letters on all four sides. A skull and crossbones stared back at them.

"Glad to get that shit off my wagon," the driver said. "I need somebody in charge to sign here." He looked around the mill yard. "Somebody white."

Samuel pulled the sheet out of his hands and signed it.

The driver raised his eyebrows while he considered the validity of that signature, then shrugged. "All right, son, can you get some men to help us unload this?" he asked.

"Cain't unload it," Wade said.

"Why the hell not?"

"This building's not finished yet. We might need to move these supplies somewheres else until it is," Wade said.

The man took a step closer to Wade. "Where's the damn office?"

"Over there," Samuel said. "But my mother will say the same thing."

"Your mother," the man said.

"Annaliese Stregal." Samuel pointed to the company sign that spanned the width of the lumber mill. "Owner."

Wade cut his eyes over at Samuel.

"It says brothers," the man said.

"No brothers. Just my mother," Samuel said. "Annaliese Stregal."

The second driver jumped off his wagon seat and stalked over. "How the hell are we supposed to get back to town?" he bellowed.

Wade kicked at the dirt. "You got horses ain't ye?"

"Four, looks like," Samuel said as he planted his feet farther apart.

"I ain't leavin' my wagons," the first man said.

"Mister, we ain't going to steal your stupid wagons," Samuel said.

"A railroad car's going back to Pinch this afternoon. Get on and we'll send the wagons back when they're empty," Wade said. "Horses, too, 'course."

Samuel threw his apple core over his shoulder.

"Shit," the man said. He headed toward the rail cars. "Well, you comin' or not?" he yelled at the other driver.

Samuel walked around the wagons. "What's all this stuff?" he asked.

"Equipment for the distillery," Wade said.

"How does a distillery work?"

"Far as I can tell, the tanbark goes into water in them vats, steeps for a while so the tannin leaches out, then that ooze goes through tubing to another cooking vat where something else happens, then it all gets boiled down to a liquor. Then you sell that to a tannery."

"How do they use this?" Samuel walked over to the skull and crossbones.

"Not sure, at the end maybe? You make sure Emeline stays away from that."

"I heard Hoyt telling somebody this tanbark collection thing is a jackass idea."

"Reckon he done run into some kind of trouble then." Wade turned to head back to his hammering.

Samuel followed him. "Why's she doing all of this? Why doesn't she just do what Papa did?" he asked.

Wade wiped his brow and led the boy to the shadow of the sawmill. "It can't keep on the way that it was, clear-cutting, leaving nothing for the future. You know how your Mama is about protecting this land."

Samuel leaned against the wall, one boot heel braced against it. "She never talks about him any more."

"Reckon it's right painful, son."

Samuel shook his head. "I miss him."

Wade cleared his throat and looked over at Tote, still driving nails. "'Course you do."

"I miss my cousins. Why did Mama have to send them to live with their aunt?"

"Their folks are gone, Sam. Your Mama's got her hands full with chillun."

"James was a pain, but at least he was a boy. Emmie follows me around all the time." Samuel picked up a rock and threw it at the dry kiln building.

"School will be startin' back up soon," Wade said.

"Yea, I guess."

Wade put his arm around the boy. "Reckon you could help me and Tote with this work? Feels right good to slam a hammer sometimes."

In the office, Annaliese and Hoyt faced each other over her desk trying to keep their voices level. Caleb leaned against the black safe, head down in careful listening, arms crossed.

Hoyt held one hand in the air to press his point. "Ma'am, it don't make no sense, this debarking idea. It kills the tree. If you want to kill a tree, we should just fell it."

"I don't want to kill trees," Annaliese said.

"Well, that's what happens when you pull off a coil of bark three feet high and lay the wood bare."

"Not necessarily," Caleb said from his corner. "Sometimes, if sprouts start below the wound—"

Annaliese threw her hands in the air. "How could you misunderstand me? I meant that we'd use the bark we scrape off here before the logs go into the millpond," Annaliese said.

Hoyt pulled a pamphlet out of his pocket and put it on the desk. He touched one index finger with the other. "First off, chestnut oak is what you want for tanbark. This here explains all that." She read the header upside down. *Department of Agriculture, bulletin 205.* "Here at the millpond, the barks get all mixed together. Second," he touched the next finger, "we don't have enough chestnut oak at one time in the mill to fool with."

"Well, what if when you find chestnut oaks while you're out in the woods, you take the bark off first, then fell the trees?" Annaliese asked.

"Ma'am, that'll slow us down," Hoyt said.

Annaliese turned the bulletin around and skimmed it, furious with herself for letting Hoyt go off half-cocked, or was she the half-cocked one? "How do you know?" she asked.

"It says so in that there bulletin. Says it takes two men half a day to peel the bark off a good size tree. And you cain't start debarking in the late afternoon expecting to finish the next morning, else the bark will bind to the tree overnight and then you cain't get it off a'tall next day. So you've got to start in the mornin' or nothin'. That's assumin' you've found a straight chestnut oak, not crooked, and on accessible land where the men can get to it and work around it."

Annaliese crossed one arm across her waist.

Hoyt planted a finger on the bulletin. "You need to leave the coils on the ground for three weeks to toughen them up enough for handling, you know, so they won't crumble when you stack them in the wagons. But if it rains on 'em, there goes your tannin." Hoyt flipped the bulletin over and stuck his finger in it again. "Then, when you collect the coils that you left in the woods for three weeks, you got to be sure to sack the bark chips that fell off the rump of the tree, because they're the richest in tannin."

"Why didn't you tell me this?" Annaliese looked over at Caleb.

"Dr. Schenck never covered this," he said in a small voice.

"And then, after all that, them leather tanners?" Hoyt said. "They'll be inspecting your distillery without notice makin' sure there's no mold in the bark. Mold injures the leather and it's hard to get rid of at the tannery." Hoyt straightened up. "Should I go on?"

Annaliese jammed her hands in her pockets and looked at him. "Well, can't y'all debark the tree after you've felled it?"

"All due respect, ma'am, are you in the timber business or the bark business?" Hoyt asked.

"Perhaps we need to talk about your tone," Annaliese said.

Hoyt raised his hands. "All due respect."

Annaliese closed her eyes. Had she taken the time to speak with any barker or tanner or distiller, she might've rethought all of this. Half a distillery up already, two wagons of equipment purchased, and now this. She had a good mind to write Schenck about his curriculum. Tears of fury pressed the backs of her eyes, but she absolutely was not going to cry in front of these men.

"Oh, just forget it," she said.

"Forget the debarking?" Hoyt said.

"The bark, the distillery, all of it," she said.

Hoyt slapped his hat on his head. "I'll tell the men."

She followed him out the door, and while Hoyt went for the mill, she headed for the distillery where Wade and Samuel pounded nails into the frame. They stopped and looked up, but she motioned to Samuel to keep going and to Wade to join her beside a wagon. He listened for a minute, raked his fingers through ropes of hair the color of a raven's wings. "Yes, ma'am, I ain't never seen 'em but I know where they are," he said. "Next county over. Union County. Hickory Mountain."

"How long would it take us to get there?"

"Two days, maybe three."

She shook her head. "Then I can't go. I can't leave for that long with all that's going on around here. Will you go?"

Deep within Wade's sweaty face, the brown eyes melted. Had she asked him to ride to Alaska, his response would've been the same. "Sure enough," he said.

"Can you leave tomorrow?" she asked. "I've already waited too long to see what's out there. I need to know their value. He's planning something. I just know it."

"First thing in the morning, then," Wade said as he caught sight of Caleb in the office doorway watching them. "Him, too, I reckon?"

"Him, too," Annaliese said. "Y'all watch your backs."

31

Caleb peered up into the canopy that towered above him at 190 feet and at the massive trunks that stretched for as far as he could see. As a lumberman's son, he called the trees yellow poplar or tulip poplar, as a forester they were *Liriodendron tulipifera*, as the grandson of a Cherokee man they were canoewood. The greenish tulip-shaped flowers that dripped from their branches as big as teacups every April had given them their nickname long before he was born. They were the tallest hardwood trees in North America, straight and free of limbs until about eighty to one hundred feet, making them all the more valuable to lumber mill owners. Even worse, the wood was known to be resistant to termites. Caleb counted the trees, seeing each one as a place in which a creature lived or raised a family or hid from talons and teeth.

A bloom of air swept through the glossy green leaves, sending them rocking into one another to catch the light and scatter shadows on the forest floor. Other than the birdsong that spilled from the canopy and the fluttering of the leaves, the forest was silent.

Wade rode up to stand beside him. "Hard to believe Mr. John didn't start with these long ago," he said. Only twenty miles away, the butchered land the two men had passed showed just how close somebody had come to these sovereigns. "Let's get on with it. You go that way, I'll go this a'way and start figgerin' how many trees we got here."

On their way home the next morning, Wade said, "I got a feelin' we just took the wrong bait."

"What do you mean?" Caleb asked.

"Black Face Mountain. We need to check on it."

When they rode up to the seedlings, the scene was as raw as entrails. Every seedling lay on the ground, chopped into bits. The men got off their horses to kick through the broken branches and trunks, none of them any longer than four feet. Across the damp earth, boot tracks circled in frenzied loops.

Caleb picked up a crushed fan of pine needles. "That man is a lunatic," he called out to Wade twenty yards away.

Wade bent down, picked something up, and headed over to show Caleb a tobacco bag with the image of an American Indian on it.

"And stupid," he said. "He stuck this in the ground with a stick to make sure we'd find it. He don't know Miss Annaliese."

32

There was no finding him. For days, Hoyt and the crews combed the hills for a sign of Dawson or his teams, but they had vanished. In town, Henry poked through the barbershop and stores to ask if anyone had heard where he'd gone, but no one had anything to offer. With crimes throughout the county more grievous than trampled seedlings to look into, the sheriff wouldn't even talk to Annaliese about investigating. She became convinced she had put the whole family in danger. Her mind would not be quiet. He was nowhere and he was everywhere. Annaliese stood on her back porch asking the adults if they smelled cigarette smoke. Nights were the worst. Every moonlit knob among the granite mounds behind her home was his bald head. Every flicker of light in the trees was the red eye of his cigarette.

Once more, she sent out men to replant Black Face Mountain, but then she had to focus on the business. The installation of the new narrow gauge railroad was going smoothly. The hiring of a driver and a mechanic, the arrival of equipment, the laying of track was on schedule and on budget. The sawyers, finally understanding that they'd no longer be pushing loaded wagons out of mud and prying logs out of rushing river currents, had a different look in their eyes when she spoke to them. At home, the kitchen scale's needle continued its tick to the right when she laid Georgia Ann in it every Sunday. The wasted bark, however, the valuable forest product that the sawyers shoveled into a firepit every day, drove Annaliese crazy. This idea, her first failure, needed to be her last failure.

One morning, Ruth blew into the office with a newspaper in her hand. Annaliese looked up from ledgers.

"Lookit this," Ruth said, dropping the *Atlanta Constitution* on her desk. Ruth put her finger on an article and photograph of a middle-aged white woman surrounded by other seated women, all holding needles above bedspreads crawling with tufted channels.

Annaliese read the headline. "Oh, yes, the chenille bedspreads. So this is the woman who's created them? Catherine Evans in Dalton, it says."

Ruth came around the desk, leaned closer to the article. "But looky here." Her finger landed on one of the seated women.

Olive. Olive in a homely dress, eyes cast down to her needle. Annaliese took a deep breath.

"Doing honest work, can you believe?" Ruth asked.

"In Dalton, just a few days' ride away."

"Oh, she won't be there long. This kinda work don't pay, Miss Annaliese. Most likely she's already done took off."

"I don't care where she is." Annaliese gave the newspaper back to Ruth and went back to the ledger. In truth, though, some days Olive was as close as Annaliese's skin.

Ruth sat down in the chair opposite her. "I seen you starin' off into space all the time," she said.

"There's been a lot going on around here, Ruth." She rubbed her eyes. "And if I could just get a good night's sleep."

"It's eatin' at you, plain as day. If you ask me, I think Olive didn't know Mr. John a'tall. She jest came here to shake you down and I want you to think so too."

"It doesn't matter anymore."

"Listen, that cousin of mine. The one named Truth? She ain't too far away. We wouldn't be gone long, 'bout an hour to get to her and an hour back."

"I'm sure she's entertaining, but—"

"It ain't for show."

Annaliese sat back and fiddled with a pencil. It had been a while since she'd been for a ride. Maybe she'd find Dawson along the way. Maybe he'd find her. Either way, she was ready. As long as her family wasn't around when she let him have it. "Where is she?"

"The other side of Turniptown Mountain."

"We have to make sure all the men—Herschel, Hoyt, Phillip—stay around the house all day."

"It's settled then," Ruth said. At the door, Ruth looked back and said, "She's a mite strange, jest so you know."

The cabin backed into a slope of land overgrown with brambles and struggling saplings, giving it the appearance of being slowly devoured by the forest. The roof was furry with sprouting things. The porch sat atop four pillars of flat rocks, slapped together like cards thrown in a pile. Chickens shot off the porch as Annaliese and Ruth rode up. Something moved in the window that had never seen a curtain.

"Truth?" Ruth called. "It's me, Ruth."

The front door opened slowly. A tangle of hair poked through the shadow, followed by shoulders, arms, and legs. Copper-colored freckles rioted across a face as pale as pastry dough. As alarming as those fiery medallions were, they were mere wallflowers under the halo of flaming red hair, the most orange red hair Annaliese had ever seen, a red that could not possibly occur in nature, and yet there it was. The volume, all wiry and wild—it sprang from the woman's scalp like a hay barn afire. When Annaliese was finally able to focus on the eyes, she saw they were moving over *her* hair and face, then up and down her body.

"Hey, Truth," Ruth said.

The eyes shifted over. "Hey, Ruth."

"Yea, well, got me a husband now. A young 'un, a wage. This here's Mrs. Stregal, the lady I work for."

Truth nodded toward Annaliese. "Figgered that."

Annaliese gave a nervous wave.

"In britches and sittin' astride that horse, no less." Truth took her time going over Annaliese's body again. "Ain't you a pretty thang."

Annaliese shifted in her saddle.

Ruth got off the horse and came closer, reins in hand. "We got somethin' to ask you 'bout."

"Figgered that, too. Only one reason anybody comes up here." Truth raised one freckled finger at the horses. "But hold on. Reckon you could take them horses over yonder? Tie 'em up agin' that tree?" She turned to look back at her window.

"Sure enough," Ruth said.

At the window, a shadow flitted by.

Truth held her door open and waved them in.

While conversation about the babies and funerals of kin filled the doorway behind her, Annaliese crept in. She could make out a bed against a wall—sprigs of hay stuck out of its mattress of amber-stained ticking—and a pair of ladder back chairs that sat at the table of weathered boards. A string of dried pumpkin rings hung beside the fireplace choked with ash and the blackened carcasses of logs. The stench of coffee, unwashed flesh, and isolation met her nostrils. There was something else, too, an unfamiliar musk. Her head turned toward the window and she found herself looking into the yellow, wary eyes of a monkey.

Ruth's gaze followed Annaliese's and she froze in the doorway. "Lord A'mighty. Where'd that come from?"

Truth said, "Oh, don't pay Sergio no mind. He's family. He don't bite. Don't like horses, though."

Sergio sent a hateful look out the window at the horses. Pom-poms swayed along the edge of his red bolero jacket embroidered with gold swirls. As soon as Truth pushed her visitors deeper into the cabin, he sprang for one of the chairs at the table.

"He showed up on my porch one day, a'starvin. Neighbor down the road told me he run off from a travelin' drummer what used him to get people to gather 'round so he could sell his castor oil and potions," Truth said.

Annaliese skirted the chairs and headed to the bed, where she sat down slowly on as few inches of it as possible, but Truth pulled a stool out from under the table for her. "Can I offer y'all somethin'? Cain't afford coffee, but got some cornbread. Cornbread maybe?" she asked, pointing to a half-empty skillet of it on the table while planting Sergio in her lap. She sent a smile to Annaliese. One tooth hung from her upper gums like a lonely stalactite in a gloomy cave.

"No," Annaliese said quickly, accepting the stool. "No, thank you." She took off her felt hat and laid it on her lap.

Truth pointed at Annaliese's blonde hair swept into a breezy bun. "How you get your hair to do like that? My hair won't do right."

"Hairpins, Truth," Ruth said, settling into the other chair. "Might think on a hairbrush, first, though."

Truth sat back. "Oh, shoot, what do I care? Hit ain't like I git callers much. Shore am glad to see y'all. Sergio is, too." She reached for a piece of cornbread, took a bite, and offered some to Sergio who took a bite, and then Truth finished it off.

As Annaliese's eyes adjusted to the dark, she could see that Sergio's jacket embroidery was actually his name in golden threads. All he needed was a small fez with a chinstrap to complete the outfit, she thought.

"He lost it, I reckon," Truth said. "He showed up with jest the jacket on, no hat."

Webs of fiery itching ran up Annaliese's neck.

"Well, ain't that somethin'," Ruth said with a more relaxed gaze upon the animal. "How'd you know his name thar?" She pointed at his jacket.

"Somebody come here who could read," Truth said.

"Mind if I open the door?" Annaliese asked.

"Sure," Truth said. "Since I learnt him a mite of English—somebody said he's Italian—he can understand me jest fine." She raked her jagged fingernails, forced into a claw by swollen knuckles, back and forth across the monkey's head. His little yellow eyes went to slits.

"So, Truth, about why we come," Ruth said.

Truth reached into a bag at the fireplace and brought out a deck of cards. "Let's have it."

Annaliese came back from the door and folded her hands on top of the table thinking witchcraft might've been better.

"See, we had this woman workin' at the house, and she up and tells Miss Annaliese here that she'd been with her husband," Ruth said.

"Huh," Truth said, looking over at Annaliese.

Annaliese had resolved to control her face no matter what, but she couldn't tell if she was succeeding or not.

"What's Mr. Happy got to say about that?" Truth asked.

"He's passed," Annaliese said, sending Ruth a look that said Shouldn't that fact have insinuated itself into Truth's brain already?

"Oh, sorry to hear that." Truth shifted in her chair. "Then why'd this woman tell her that? Wait. She wanted money, right?" Truth asked.

Annaliese cut her eyes at Ruth, who looked relieved that Truth had gotten something right. "Yea, and Miss Annaliese gave her some and she's done took off, but the thing is Miss Annaliese is wantin' to know if it's true."

"Well, y'all have come to the right place." Truth shuffled the cards and divided them into two stacks that she pushed toward Annaliese. "They say self brag's half a scandal, but I'm good at figurin' that out. I get this all the time. Cut them cards." Truth pushed back a spray of red hair and again studied Annaliese's face with an appraising eye. Sergio cocked his head at her, left, right, left. For Annaliese, squirming on the stool against wobbly nail heads and going over recipes and the Farmer's Almanac to block any more thoughts from being snatched up, the four-eyed scrutiny went on for eternity. She split the stack in two and pushed them back. Truth turned them face up.

A mucousy cough rattled through Truth's chest while she looked at the cards, at Annaliese, at the window, then down at Sergio. His yellow eyes barely above the table edge—all that was visible of the monkey—watched Annaliese, and she saw in those eyes a capacity for comprehension beyond that of many of her employees.

Truth reached for Annaliese's hand. "This woman. Name starts with a P sound."

A frown slipped past Annaliese.

"No, wait. That ain't right. Hit's a'comin' to me now. Her name's from the Bible?" Truth's grip on Annaliese's fingers tightened as if to squeeze the information out of her. Annaliese wiggled them away with a shake of her head. "Oh, never mind that," Truth said. She closed her eyes. "But I can see her, sure enough. She's got big titties, tits like two puppies in a poke." Truth opened one eye.

Ruth shot a look at Annaliese and turned back to Truth. "Do you see her with Mr. John?"

Sergio climbed onto the table, walked carefully around the cards, and sat in front of Annaliese, who leaned back to show him that her hat already occupied her lap. The nailheads on her stool grew taller, harder.

"Wait, wait, I see them kissin' on your back porch," Truth said.

"Naw, you don't," Ruth said.

Truth leaned back in her chair and threw the cards in the air. "Listen. Bein' in my line of work, I seen a lot of this. Here's what I got to say to you, Mizz Stregal. He married you, supported and protected you, gave you children." A wave of panic washed over her face. "I reckon you got children? Did I get that right?"

Annaliese nodded. Blood raced from her chest to her neck to her eyes.

"Look," Truth said. "Parts is parts. Women parts and menfolk parts. Menfolk just want a warm place to put their almighty precious part, and they don't think a thing about it. I know them ain't the rules, but that's men. He loved you, right? Loved your children? Didn't go out to feed the hogs and never come back, right? Ain't that what you really wanted?"

Annaliese nodded, as did Ruth as she reached for her hand across the table.

Truth looked at the two leaning toward each other. "Now wait a minute." She pointed a claw at them. "You two, you ain't family, I know, but you got somethin' there. Some kinda blood joinin' you. I see somethin' family-like you share, somethin' nary a soul else knows," Truth said.

"I was nursin' her baby," Ruth said.

Truth's gaze slid to Annaliese's breasts. "That ain't it," she said. "Somethin' else."

A chicken walked in and headed for a nest in a corner. Sergio's head moved left to right, as though he was reading the visitors' faces. With one of her gnarly fingers, Truth dug out a strand of hair and twirled it. "Somethin' goin' on here. Strange," Truth said.

Ruth rose from her chair. "Awright, then. Reckon we'll be goin'. Thank ye."

Annaliese laid a dollar on the table, which Sergio picked up and stuffed into his jacket, followed by a tip of the fez that wasn't there.

"Hope y'all will come back," Truth said. "I'd be all tore up if I didn't see you again, ma'am."

"Bye, now," Annaliese said. She crossed herself and pushed Ruth toward the door, with one eye on Sergio who had leapt for the windowsill to screech at the horses.

Truth stood up. "Hold on," she said as she grabbed Ruth by the shoulders and turned her sideways.

"Whatever you're seein', it better be good news. I'm all tore up right now," Ruth said.

"Yea, well, I reckon it's good, but that depends on how you feel about it."

"What is it?" Annaliese pulled Ruth away from the claws.

Truth pointed at Ruth's belly. "A bun in the oven, that's what."

Ruth's knees gave way.

"Yep, I see another baby on the way. Give it another month or so, and I reckon you'll find your monthlies ain't come back." Truth looked at the two hopefully, as if expecting another dollar, but they didn't move. Annaliese and Ruth were frozen to the doorway, to each other, steadying themselves as they absorbed all that this could mean if it were true.

Truth watched them. "Strange," she said again. "Why are you two holdin' on to each other like you jest seen Jesus' empty tomb?"

"Are you sure? She's nursing her baby," Annaliese said. "No monthlies with nursing."

Truth shook her head. "That ain't it. There's another baby," she said.

"Ruth?" Annaliese asked. "How do you feel?"

"I don't feel no different," Ruth said. "My bleedin's never been regular."

They went down the steps on unsteady legs, holding onto each other, untying reins and climbing into saddles to carry home yet another secret between them, one that in time, if true, could possibly set them free.

33

A slow tide of clouds rolled over the mountaintops on the morning of the day Annaliese had chosen. Standing at her bedroom window, she watched them move across the restless gray sky, not the glorious weather she'd hoped for. Today was the day, though, and she owned that decision. Whether she was going to feel glorious tonight, who knew, but she wasn't turning back. Henry had said no more about his cabin and their future, hadn't even reached to hold her hand, which took the pressure off and gave her a chance to think. About him. About his body. About what she wanted. With every decision she made for the company, Annaliese felt the intoxication of being in charge of what happened in her life, the thrill of driving her life events instead of being mowed down by them. Today she was going to drive. Today was the full symphony or nothing.

Standing before her mirror, chin cupped in hand, she turned her face to one side then the other and wondered whether she could still be called lovely. Her hair was as dry as straw, her face was tanned and lined, the modulated voice that had charmed friends in Louisville parlors, gone. Had she become too rough? The man waiting for her downstairs didn't seem to think so.

She pulled open the bureau's bottom drawer to withdraw a wooden box tied with twine and stamped *Federation Internationale de La*

Regeneration Humaine, 27 Rue de la Duee, Paris – xx. She locked the door. A few minutes later, she pulled on her underpants and trousers and went downstairs.

Henry's horse led them through the June woods of leaf mats sodden with the night's rain. Annaliese rocked along behind, savoring the smell of moist earth and honeysuckle and trying not to watch for Dawson around every bend. She focused on Henry's broad back, the black hair escaping his hat, his swaying shoulders. Why hadn't they done this more often, a casual ride for the two of them when bellies at home were full and no one there expected them back for a while, the kind of open-ended ride where anything could happen between two people in the richness of boundless time.

She knew this glen well, could've managed it on a moonless night, but she let him choose the place to stop. As he tied up their horses near a stream, he looked at the gray clouds gravid with threat.

"We probably shouldn't stay long," Henry said.

"Oh, pooh, Henry. We might not see a drop," Annaliese said with a smile.

They took a basket and quilt from the saddlebags and settled beside the water to poke through the meal, ignoring thunder's muffled rattling. For a while, she let the conversation amble along the paths of their buoyant lives—Georgia Ann's growth, Caleb's contributions, Henry's clients and his verdicts won, but she was barely listening. She tapped his boot with hers. Finally, he leaned in to kiss her lightly. She kissed him back, ran her fingers through the thick black hair she'd been watching all morning, inhaled his smell. With her hands on his shoulders, she pulled him down to the quilt for even better kissing. He raised up and went back to talking, talking, talking. As the tingling in her breasts seeped away, he talked of the future— five, ten, twenty years out—and where even greater happiness could lie if they were together. Man and wife together. That would be happiness enough, he said, no matter what life threw at them for the rest of their lives.

Annaliese sat up, heart pounding in her chest for the wrong reason. Man and wife?

"Well?" Henry said. "How 'bout it, Anna. Will you marry me?"

Marry?! He hadn't even kissed her for a month.

"Isn't that what you want?" he asked.

Of course, she thought. Henry thought this was what she was waiting for. Or maybe he just felt that it was the honorable thing to do at this stage. But to her, marriage meant decisions shared, privacy invaded, a new layer of obligations, new relatives to get used to. Relatives! She'd never met any of his. A husband would expect to have equal say, more than equal say probably, oh yes, even Henry. And who was to say that the balance of power wouldn't shift imperceptibly, a little bit every day, and then one day there she'd be again, back in the sidecar. When she was a girl, men made things happen. Nowadays, women made things happen too. Annaliese liked making things happen.

In running the business, she'd learned that sometimes it was better to smile or frown than commit to words. In this case, she decided it was better to just kiss. She pulled him back down to the quilt. As his kisses landed faster on her face, her ears, her neck, he pushed her jacket collar open to get to more skin. *Finally!* her brain screamed as his lips raced up and down her neck. But again he came up for air and went back to his propped right arm. She wanted to knock it out from under him. He started talking again. She unbuttoned her jacket, tapped her finger to her collarbone with a smile, and Henry went after it. He was on top of her. She felt her hips rising to meet his, felt his stiff penis precisely above the place where it was going to feel so good in a few minutes. She was relieved to find that despite the beating that region had taken during childbirth, all of the right nerve endings had just ignited. They throbbed expectantly in that warm, wet place where she had inserted the French pessary that morning. Her body throbbed with all of the desire she'd been squelching since she first laid eyes on him two years ago, the evening he rode up to her porch where she waited with John, hoisted one leg over the saddle, and landed in her front yard hard and sure.

Henry's hands ran up and down her overwrought body. Her pelvis joined her brain in wishing they would move over to the buttons on her trousers. The frantic lover moaned above her, grinding his hips into her. And yet—he rolled off again. He threw his arm over his eyes. "Sorry," he said. "I shouldn't have done that."

She groaned. A gust of wind rustled the treetops, and small pebbles of rain swept in.

"We should go," he said, taking his arm off his face.

That. Is. It. she thought.

She rubbed his shoulder, and when he finally turned his body toward her, she made circles on his chest. Her circles got bigger—down to his belt buckle, up to his neck and back down past the buckle, then farther, then the rubbing began, and finally, as Henry lay there as frozen as a young preacher in the wrong part of town, she took his hand and put it inside her jacket to land directly, unmistakably, intentionally on her Catholic breast. He caressed it gently, then less so, then watched wide-eyed as she arched her back with pleasure.

"Really?" Henry asked.

Annaliese took off her jacket and started unbuttoning her fly. Henry worked out of his jacket, shirt, and pants. Their hands slid over each other's skin, slippery and musky from the soft rain. She was accustomed to selfish hands in a hurry, but Henry's were blessedly slow as they explored the swell of her hips and breasts. He seemed to know that every stroke, every cupping of bottom and breast, was another log on the fire, a fire he wanted to give her.

"Not yet," she said.

Annaliese playfully pushed him off and onto his back. Oh, the arousal of aggression! Her kisses began at his nipples that smelled of salty sweat, then moved down to his belly, and down to the tangle of curly hair with a different kind of smell, then the mushroom cap staring up at her, purple and shiny. She slid her hand over it—Henry's moan startled the horses— and took her first up close look at an erect penis. A turgid blue vein snaked down the shaft to the twin sacs nestled in black hair, pink and balloonish. No red spots. Plunging on, she stroked them, marveling at their rubbery ridges. "How's this?" she asked. "You like this?"

Henry was looking down at her, flabbergasted. "Lord A'mighty, yes," he said, "but come here."

The rain began lashing the trees as she wiggled back into his arms. Branches heaved and scratched at one another. Henry touched and explored her body until he pushed apart her thighs with his knees and entered her. She gasped at the burn, but then it burned less and less with each thrust, and the glory of him inside her simply took over. As his chest pressed down, he placed her hands above her head and folded his fingers into hers, as if to say *Come with me to this place we both want so very badly.* Henry moved in and out slowly, shifted around, and she realized he was searching for the right spot for *her*. She started trying to find it, too, with a tiny shift of the hips here, a dip and scoop there. In a few minutes, her muscle spasms told both of them they'd found it, so he let go. Each wave between her legs was stronger than the one before, and when she thought she couldn't pull Henry into her any deeper, a release like she had never known shot through every cell. Her body shuddered with pleasure at long last. Her heartbeat pounded in her ears. Raindrops raced sideways over their bodies, blinding them even more. When they opened their eyes, Henry pulled the quilt over them, tucked her under his chin, and said, "I love you, Anna."

She looked up into his eyes. "I love you too, Henry," she said, and it was true.

The last of the rain raced away to the next mountain, and the air grew ragged and cold. As they pulled soaked clothes back on, she realized that Henry hadn't liked her fingers on his nipples. In fact, he'd pushed them away, as if her fiddling was annoying. Before today, she hadn't had the experience to know if John's arousal with the tugging was unique, but now she did know that it wasn't common to all men, giving Olive's claim about John a sliver more of credence.

34

Ruth closed the parlor's pocket doors and hurried to the mirror on the wall. With quick fingers, she unbuttoned the top of her dress, pulled down her shift, and looked at the breasts still recovering from being squeezed over a cup an hour ago. Somehow, she'd coaxed out almost an ounce. Dorothy said that was more than enough. Leaning in, Ruth looked hard at the pale pink halos around her nipples. Were they darker, was the burning question. She squinted hard, as if that would change them to the near-purple that had been the earliest sign of her last pregnancy weeks before two missed monthlies. But they were still the same washed-out pink they were an hour ago.

She switched her attention to the creamy skin upon which the halos rode. Annaliese had taught her before that dark blue veins under the translucent skin would be another sign, the blood supply for two. With a breast nearly mashed into the mirror, she was thinking that maybe the veins were that expectant blue when the front door slammed. A gust of air swept under the pocket doors. Ruth hurried to fasten buttons. Emeline yanked open the doors.

"What're you doing?" the girl asked.

Ruth got the last button fastened and turned around. "Checkin' on some bug bites," she said. "Well, looky thar, where'd you find that?"

Emeline thrust a frog at Ruth. "In the springhouse." The frog's bloated white belly was as swollen as an udder three hours past milking time. It managed two croaks, legs quivering with the effort. "He ate all of our butter," she said.

"So that's where it's been goin'. You jest take him right back on outside." Ruth sat down on the rug to fold a thick square of fabric—yellow daisies flung across a sea of blue—in half.

Emeline put the toad on its back next to Ruth's sewing basket. The green legs swam through the air.

"Look at me, Emmie," Ruth said. "Since yore Mama done taught me to read, I can use a pattern." She swept away wrinkles, checked that the right sides were together and selvages were squared. Out of a white envelope she pulled a packet of brown papers, thin as butterfly wings, with shaking hands. Unfolding them, she tore a corner.

"Uh, oh," Emeline said. "What's wrong?"

"Just excited is all, 'bout bein' able to read these here papers." Ruth smoothed her hand over a square of the tissue paper, squinted at the black dotted lines that indicated basting stitches, darts, and seam allowances.

"But you already know how to sew," Emeline said, sitting down beside her.

"Ain't never used a pattern, though. Lookit all the different dresses it makes."

"Can I help?" Emeline asked.

"Sure, baby." Ruth pulled a pincushion out of the basket. "I'll be pinning these papers to the fabric. When I need a pin, you give me one." She tied the pincushion to the child's wrist.

Ruth's scissors got busy working around the pattern pieces for a skirt, a yoke, the cuffs and sleeves. She laid the skirt piece on the fold of the fabric as the black arrows commanded, and fit the others around what was left. Ruth wiggled her fingers at Emeline to be given pins, and began rocking them through paper and fabric.

"Ouch," Ruth said, rearing up from her work. She shoved her finger in her mouth.

"You stick yourself?"

"M'hands are shakin' so bad," Ruth said. "Hand me another one."

Emeline handed her a pin. "You already made me a dress out of this," she said.

"This here's for Lucy."

"At least it's not for Georgia Ann. Everything's for the baby." Emeline jammed a pin in and out of the cushion.

Ruth sat back on her heels. How well she understood that sentiment. How often she prayed to accept the fact that one particular child in the household would likely always hold all the keys. Emeline's face broke her heart. For Ruth, witnessing her children's pain—for Sam and Emmie were as much her children as Annaliese's—was always worse than bearing it herself. She scooted back to lean against a chair and tugged on Emeline until she toppled into her lap. She untied the grubby ribbon at the bottom of her braid and worked it apart, spreading the strands across Emeline's shoulders. With slow, firm pulsing, Ruth's fingertips traveled across the child's scalp.

"Baby, you know you got more dresses than you'll ever need," Ruth said.

Emeline huffed into Ruth's lap. They both knew this wasn't about dresses.

The sound of the sawmill's noon whistle floated uphill to the open window. The saws started winding down. Annaliese would be coming in the front door soon, as planned.

"You remember last year when we found them baby rabbits whose mama got taken by the fox?" Ruth asked.

Emeline rolled over and whispered the names she'd given the five despite her mother's forbidding her to do so.

"Remember how helpless they was?" Ruth asked.

"We fed them and kept them in the warming drawer of the stove."

"Until they was grown enough to take care of themselves."

"They were so soft." Emeline stroked the long gone Hoppy now curled on Ruth's knee. "We let them go on Bunny Mountain."

"Well, what do you reckon would've happened to them if we hadn't taken them in, them poor little things?"

Emeline's hand went still.

"Now, Emmie, we both know some critters need extra help to get full grown, don't we?"

Emeline released a sigh worthy of the stage.

"Your mama's worried about your sister. You know that."

The child teared up. "Uh huh."

In the hall, Dorothy was calling for Ruth. A baby's crying followed her calls.

Ruth scrambled to her feet, pulling Emeline up with her.

Dorothy arrived in the doorway with a fussy Georgia Ann squirming in her arms. "Ready?" She held a copper cup in one hand.

"But Miss Annaliese ain't here yet," Ruth said, going to the door to look.

"We'll tell her what happens. Come on," Dorothy said, holding the cup out to her.

"I cain't do it, my hands are shakin' too much," Ruth said.

They hurried to the kitchen, with Emeline trailing along asking why the fuss over this feeding, why that cup, why did she need Ruth?

Dorothy got settled in a chair and put the cup of Ruth's milk to Georgia Ann's lips. A few drops went in. The baby hesitated at the taste, blinked as she swallowed. Ruth hovered, hands sliding up and down her apron. Again Dorothy put the cup to the baby's mouth and tilted it so a tiny stream of milk flowed in. The baby smacked her lips around the milk, spit it out, and turned her head away in clear refusal.

"Ruth," Dorothy whispered. "Look at that."

"You sure that's my milk?"

"Yes, of course I'm sure. We put it in this copper cup, remember? I took it out of the icebox just now."

Ruth's hands flew to her face.

"What?" Emeline asked as she looked back and forth. "Why are you crying, Ruth?"

"We got to go tell Miss Annaliese," Ruth said between sobs.

"What?" Emeline tugged on her aunt's sleeve. "Tell her what?"

The baby wailed with hunger, but Dorothy just jiggled her. "Ruth's going to have a baby, Emmie. Georgia Ann won't drink her milk because it tastes funny. This is what happens when a nursing mother has another one on the way."

Emeline clamped her hands over her ears. "Then give her somebody else's milk!"

The front door slammed. Annaliese came running down the hall, stopping at the sight. "Well?" she asked.

"She won't take it, Anna," Dorothy said.

"Ruth's going to have a baby, Mama," Emeline shouted.

"Lord, Lord," Ruth said. "Can it be true?"

Annaliese grabbed Ruth by the shoulders. Equals for the moment in relief and guarded hope, they looked into each other's eyes. All that a pregnancy could mean passed between them like a lifetime sentence lifted. Only God would know the truth, but now there was possibility to cling to and a choice to make as to how to think about Lucy when their eyes fell on her for the rest of their lives.

35

On the first day of July, the entire Stregal household and Henry gathered in Annaliese's kitchen. Ruth stirred a pot on the stove while Dorothy stood next to her, bowl in hand. Emeline fussed at Samuel to hurry up and sit down in the chair that Mr. Chastain held for him. Annaliese put Georgia Ann in her brother's arms, which prompted her to smack her lips and look around for a cup. She and everyone who fed her had mastered the cup and dribble, but at three months, Georgia Ann was only fourteen pounds. It was time to move on to solids.

The Atlanta surgeon had explained to Annaliese on Henry's telephone that yes, solid food going past a cleft palate sometimes came out the nose, but that didn't seem to bother most children, so she should try. He understood Annaliese's anxiety over Georgia Ann's poor growth, but she was too young for the surgery that would close the palate and lips. He preferred to wait until ten months of age, when speech was developing.

"I thought I just had to get her to ten pounds," she cried.

"Who told you that?" the surgeon asked. "Ten months."

He went on to say that several surgeries would be necessary, but really, he couldn't say more until he examined the baby. Meantime, by all means, feed her. Annaliese spent a long time on the telephone with the doctor, straining to detect expertise in his voice, not that she would know it when she heard it. He talked of closing nasal and oral cavities, making incisions in nose and lip, and suturing. Kindness, though, she'd heard that clearly, so kindness plus his reputation and her prayers would have to be enough. She was feeling better until he said, "The surgery is a long and bloody one, so the stronger the baby is when we operate, the better. Get some weight on her." After she hung up, she burst into tears.

Ruth poured a stream of grits into the pink rosebud bowl that Dorothy held out to her. Dorothy stirred and blew furiously, and gave it to Annaliese. Touching a dab to her lips until it cooled, she offered a spoonful to Georgia Ann, squirming in Samuel's lap. The baby gummed the pearly mush for a few seconds, worked her confused tongue around it, and spit it all out. Samuel and Emeline squealed with laughter. The baby pumped her arms and legs and looked up at her mother for more. The next dab went in, the tongue curled and the lips smacked, and as Annaliese leaned in for a closer look, the baby sneezed it all over her. The children laughed again, but the adults exchanged terse looks. Annaliese wiped the baby's nose clear, took a deep breath, and spooned up an even tinier amount.

"Let me, let me," Emeline cried.

Annaliese blew on the spoon and gave it to Emeline. The mush went in, rolled around the tongue, came back out. Undaunted, Georgia Ann reached for the spoon.

The third time, after getting it all down she began flailing with choking. Annaliese pounded on her back, stroked the baby's nostrils until a slimy stream came out. Georgia Ann let out one furious scream and then stopped breathing. Her face went red, redder, and while everyone begged for another scream, her life—all life in that kitchen—hung in the stifling air. Georgia Ann stared at her mother, as if deciding whether to ever inhale again. Her family leaned in, impotent and frantic. Finally, the baby threw her head back and filled her lungs, cried hard for a minute, then less hard, and looked around for the spoon. Emeline sent a questioning look at her mother, who dipped the spoon once more into the grits and handed it to Emeline. The confused tongue got most of it down, but she went to choking again. Annaliese pulled her out of Samuel's arms, and with pats on her back and the calmest assurances she could muster, took her outside to the garden.

They walked through the corn stalks to look at the broad, rough blades and dewy silks that sprouted from what Ruth called the roastin' ears. A nation of ladybugs worked back and forth across the green skins. Georgia Ann pondered these meandering black specks as she blinked away her tears. A couple of grits rode the glistening snot stream coming out of her nose. Annaliese plucked a leaf from the green bean vine and wiped it. They moved on through the rows of beans, okra, and turnips, with Annaliese naming them and Georgia Ann reaching. Together, they lifted the broad leaves of pumpkin vine to check on the little green orbs that suckled on the fat mother vein. In the final row, another vine of green leaves spread out luxuriously and Annaliese explained that in this case, the goods were hidden. Irish potatoes were a matter of faith, she said.

The baby began whimpering. The chubby fist went to her mouth. Surrounded by food, the child was starving.

The sound of someone coming through the corn stalks made Annaliese turn around. "Let's try again," Henry said. He cupped the baby's head in his hands. "She'll figure it out."

As they turned back toward the house, Annaliese looked again at the potato vine and thought of the life it nurtured below ground, unseen but growing, as the vine collected sunshine and rain on its unstoppable timetable.

36

In mid-July, when all the crops in the county had been picked and sold, gallons of corn liquor had been funneled into jugs, and cash into people's pockets, the merchants of Pinch stood ready at their counters. Drummers flocked into town to sell dishware, tonics, and lightning rods out of the back of their chaotic wagons. Meddling's boarding house teemed with diners and the Meddling relatives who had been conscripted for the month. Down the street at Smith's Mercantile, the washboards in the window were sold as soon as they were placed on the red fabric Mrs. Smith had strategically chosen in imitation of a Mr. Woolworth, widely known for his belief that red stimulated buying.

Into the bustling town Annaliese and Caleb arrived one Saturday afternoon, hours later than they'd planned but still with enough daylight for their return. They found a hitching post and split off, agreeing to meet in front of the barbershop in two hours. Annaliese headed for Henry's office, where she signed documents that put the two hundred acres of tulip poplars in a conservation trust. Afterward, they stood in a line at Meddling's waiting for a table. People on their way out stopped to chat, and with each conversation that was opened by people whose stomachs were already full, Annaliese became more blatant about looking around them to the dining room where the servers didn't seemed to be in a hurry either. Diners lingered in conversation over the dirty plates. Henry patted her shoulders. When Thessalonia sidled up to them, he gave her a meaningful look, and she seated them shortly.

After they ordered, a thin man in buckskin pants and homespun shirt walked up to their table.

"Help you?" Henry said as he got up from his chair.

"Looking for Mrs. Stregal?"

Annaliese looked up at the man. Young and lean, he looked like a strip of beef jerky. "Yes?" she said.

"My name is Lamar McDowell, ma'am," he said. "I own a small lumber company."

"Sir, we're having dinner here," Henry said. "Can this wait?"

McDowell put his hand on Annaliese's chair. His jaw worked hard under the whiskers. "I was wondering if you'd want to sell some of your land, being a widow and all?" he asked.

Annaliese looked at the skittish eyes peering down at her, the chewed fingernails, the filthy shirt, and doubted that he owned anything more valuable than his boots. The smell of tobacco smoke came off him like a noxious fog.

Her eyes went hard. "And which land is that?" she asked, though she knew.

"That nice stand of poplars and oaks on your property over in Union County, ma'am." He kept his voice low.

"He sent you, didn't he?"

"Who?"

"No." She leaned forward to get away from his hand on her chair, but he didn't budge.

Henry stepped toward the man, showed him the door.

McDowell leaned down and lowered his voice again. "Twenty five thousand dollars for all of it."

Annaliese shot out of her chair. "You tell Buck Dawson—"

"Who?" McDowell said again. His Adam's apple bobbed with his anxious swallowing.

"Dawson. I knew he'd show up again. Where is he? You tell him—"

"Nobody sent me but my pappy, ma'am."

Annaliese crossed her arms. "What's the name of your outfit?" she asked.

"McDowell Lumber, ma'am."

"Never heard of it."

"It's in South Carolina."

She stepped forward. "How much log makes up a board foot?"

"One foot long, one foot wide, one inch thick."

She nodded. "Name the hardwood factory grades."

"Uh, prime."

Suspicion grew in her eyes. "And?" she asked. There were five more that anyone with a pappy in the lumber business would've learned by the age of ten.

With a nervous look at all of the diners now leaning into his conversation, McDowell said, "All right, look. How about twenty-seven thousand?"

"You can tell Mr. Dawson that that land is in a trust now. Tell everybody you know."

McDowell stepped back. "What's that mean?"

"It means she can't sell it," Henry said. "She can't cut it either."

"Not never?"

"Never," Annaliese said.

Fear swept through McDowell's eyes—Annaliese saw it quite clearly—and he took a deep breath. He turned and wove his way through the tables to the hall. The dining room was silent. Everyone watched him go.

Henry said, "Did you see how scared he was?"

"Yes." Annaliese was already putting her napkin on the table.

Henry got up from his chair at the same time. "I think you should get on home and I'm coming with you."

An hour later at the bank, Annaliese stood in a line that crawled toward the teller's cage. At the mercantile, she turned away in exasperation from the crowded counters to be at the barbershop on time, but as she walked up, she saw that there was no Caleb. She sat on the whittlers' bench ignoring looks from the whittlers and spitters. The courthouse clock chimed three times.

Henry walked up, saddlebags in hand, and sat down beside her.

"I shouldn't have left the house today. I knew it." She wagged her foot. "Where is Caleb?"

"If he's not here in a few minutes, we'll leave without him," Henry said.

At three fifteen, Caleb walked up with packages under both arms, complaining about the line at the post office until he saw the looks on their faces. "What happened?" he asked.

"We think Dawson's back," Henry said. "We need to get on home."

They lost more minutes tying the packages to horses that grew antsy with the hurrying and yelling all around them. The sun began its descent toward the treetops as the three riders began their climb into the hills. While they still dared, they kicked the horses into trotting. Each minute laid a deeper hue on the brooding forms all around. No one spoke. Only the haunting refrains of whippoorwills and the sound of hooves kicking up rocks broke the quiet. The wrung out light forced them to slow down and pick their way around holes and fallen branches. Finally, they spotted their landmark, the granite knob that meant the sawmill was half a mile away.

A rifle shot pierced the night. The riders took off into the stretch they hoped the horses remembered well enough, and as they were leaning into the turn before the sawmill, they ran into the smell of smoke. Seconds later, they raced into the mill yard.

The sawmill was on fire, all of it, every wall and roof timber. Flames licked the corners of the first of twenty stacks of processed timber in the mill yard. Next in line was the commissary, then the wooden frame of the half-built distillery, and the wagons stacked with crates of equipment. Annaliese looked up the hill at her home and saw two figures running down the road, rifles in hand. Samuel and Phillip. Kicking her horse to get to them, she motioned to Caleb to let the mules out of the corral. Another rifle shot rang out. Henry stopped her and pointed.

Herschel was running toward the woods at the mill yard's edge, shooting wildly at a man heading for the forest. Herschel stopped, fired again, sending dirt spraying near the man's boots, but the man slipped into the pines. He lowered his rifle and held his hand out to stop Samuel and Phillip from coming any closer. They turned toward the fire bursting with fury across the buildings. Annaliese screamed at them, but the din of roof beams crashing and mules braying buried her cries. Everyone stood rooted to the ground, trying to decide where to go, whether to go, what might be saved and how. The fire buckets and shovels were in the sawmill.

Caleb struggled to lift the corral gate latch that bulged under the crush of frantic mules. Samuel shot out of Phillip's grip to help, deaf to his mother's commands to stop. As her son crossed the yard, Annaliese saw a rifle swing out from under one of the distillery equipment wagons. Gilded by the flames, its barrel was unmistakably following the boy. Annaliese jumped off the horse, pulled her Winchester out of its leather pouch, and leveled it at the dark place under the wagon, an impossible target.

The shooter fired and Samuel hit the ground, covering his head with his hands. Annaliese blasted at the dark place, the wagon bed, the crates it held, coming back from each wicked kick of the buttstock to aim and fire again at the wagon and its lethal cargo that would stop the shooter if her bullets did not. Spent cartridges flew from her elbows in all directions.

The rifle barrel swung toward her, fired twice into the smoke, then fell to the ground.

Two hands came out from under the wagon, bringing out a bald head and the shoulders of Buck Dawson crawling on his belly, eyes closed, screaming. He clutched his head, rolled over, and dug his fingers into the black craters on his head. Annaliese ran to Samuel and helped him up, and while the other men scanned the shadows for more shooters, mother and son ran to Henry, just ahead of the mules thundering past.

Dawson took off for the millpond behind the raging sawmill. Everyone followed, dodging timbers crashing down. Ripping off his shredded shirt, Dawson staggered toward the water shimmering orange with the reflections of the flames. He tried to push a floating trunk away from the edge to get at the water. When it wouldn't move, he scrambled over it and jumped into the water. He came back up screaming even louder, clawing at the eyes that were blind to another log that he had set in motion. Like a wolf on a fawn, it crept closer to Dawson on the deadly tide of his own making, closing the gap between that log and the one behind him, the gap that was about to be the last air that Buck Dawson would ever breathe.

They watched the top of Dawson's head disappear behind a glistening log that bobbed calmly forward. A hand shot up to claw at it, shudder, and slip below the sky of timber slowly forming silently above. Hoyt ran up with shovels, glanced at the water that he understood was doing its violent work, and pulled Caleb and Phillip away to dig dirt and fight what flames they could.

Henry held Annaliese by the shoulders and she held Samuel by his. As the flames roared behind them and the sawmill crumbled to the ground, the three waited for the water to go still, to see nothing, not a head or a hand or a ripple, across the orange water.

37

By mid-morning, everyone within fifteen miles had come to gawk. With somber faces, the sawyers and stumpers and railroad workers came up to Annaliese to murmur condolences and their promises to rebuild. Their wives prayed with her, touched her shoulders, and swept her children into their arms while they all stared at what still stood—the saws, the railroad cars, and the black safe that had dominated the corner of the office. Within those impervious iron walls, her company, on paper at least, had survived. Once again, John's foresight had protected her while devastation swept through.

The sheriff kicked at a smoldering sawmill beam that had been the frame of the door to the millpond. With the ashen Dawson lying face down at the edge of the pond, his rifle under the splintered distillery wagon, and his horse tied up down the road, the sheriff simply nodded. There was little discussion about who was responsible.

Within hours, the sawyers had started making good on their word. Their shovels and pickaxes got busy scraping charred timbers into a pile. Someone rounded up the mules, and a deputy arrived to load Dawson's body into a wagon. As it rattled away, Annaliese kept the children at a distance from the ghoulish face and the burned scalp and shoulders, but she did not pull them away. She had tried to never shield them from any of the truths of this harsh life. She grabbed Henry's shirt still stinking with smoke and buried her face in it. None of them had slept or changed their clothes.

On the day that the last of the waste had been burned and the warped equipment hauled away, the family gathered around the dining room table. Samuel spread a roll of paper across it. Emeline climbed into a chair to put forks and knives at the corners. The four adults pulled the chairs away for a closer look at the wobbly drawings—a crude building with a row of windows like the sawmill's, a pond behind it like the sawmill had (now with ducks in it), lumpy mules standing stiff-legged in a corral, train tracks, and numerous other buildings large and small. Stick figures with beards walked from one to other. A happy sun face smiled down on all.

"Here's where the new dry kiln will go," Samuel said, pointing. "We moved it away from the commissary."

"Sounds good," Henry said.

The adults nodded their heads as they made out what was what. "Looks like a good plan," Phillip said. It was more or less the same as the old one.

"And there's a horseshoe pit here," Samuel said. "See?" A dotted line marked out a rectangle behind the commissary. The adults realized that the two black squiggles on its opposite ends that looked like sticks were, in fact, stakes.

"This is for us," Samuel said as he looked up at his mother for a nod, which she gave. "And the sign here," he pointed to the sawmill, "will say Stregal Family Lumber Company," Samuel said. He scanned faces for a reaction.

"A bully idea," Henry said. He looked over at Annaliese, fighting back tears.

"We left out the distillery, right Mama?" Samuel asked, pointing to the spot where the beginnings of the original had stood.

Annaliese winced. "Oh, don't remind me," she said.

Henry straightened up from his leaning over the drawing. "I've been thinking about that. What if you told the sawyers' wives and other women out there that they can collect the bark and sell it?"

Annaliese took her hand off her face. "They could come behind Hoyt and the crew," she said.

"Their children could help," Henry said.

"Then they could sell it to the distillers themselves."

"Make a little cash money."

Everyone watched this back and forth without a word, some comprehending more than others the significance of Henry's contribution.

"If their children helped, they could have a tree skinned in no time," Annaliese said as she put her hands on the table. "Then they could be out of Hoyt's way quick. What a great idea."

Henry paused and leaned forward to meet her gaze. "I do have them every now and then, you know."

38

Atlanta's Union Station pulsed with the energy of a thousand destinations, geographical and envisioned. The noise assaulted Annaliese's ears that had been softened by raindrops and the whispering of boughs. Train engines screeched into their docks to wait with hissing respirations for the next crowd. Every traveler, burdened with bags or children or deadlines or all three, pushed past her with the city brusqueness she'd forgotten. In a way, she liked their disinterest in her and the baby in her arms. Too many stares at them on the train ride south to Atlanta had stoked her anxiety. Henry took her elbow to guide her through the throng to the street. Phillip followed with a porter and their bags.

Her last phone call to the surgeon had left her again in tears, this time the happiest kind. When she told him Georgia Ann was twenty pounds at nine months, he congratulated her. An assistant came on the line to schedule the surgery in four weeks.

Henry pulled his coat tighter and waved toward the line of taxis outside. One chugged toward them in a fit of combustion. "Piedmont Hotel," Henry said to the driver. He and Phillip stuffed bags into the boot, and everyone climbed in.

Annaliese looked out her window at the granite-paved streets and the trolleys tethered to electric lines. She noted that the streetlamps were missing the metal arms at the top for the lamplighter's ladder, which meant that the comfort of flickering gaslight at night had been swept aside by the cold steady beam of electric lights. The city, still rebuilding after Tecumseh Sherman's holocaust she supposed, gave off a swaggering, youthful air. Modern, stone-faced office buildings rose floor upon floor to the sky, some filling an entire block, as did the Piedmont Hotel. When they pulled up to the entrance, she gaped at it until a valet opened her door.

Henry and Phillip got in line at the registration desk, leaving Annaliese to wander the lobby, bouncing the hungry baby in her arms to jolly her until they got into their room. Passing towering palms that fanned against marble columns, she arrived at the dining room, where money gleamed in quiet strength. A sea of white linen-draped tables, all but two occupied, encircled a bubbling fountain. Heavy damask drapes and Persian rugs absorbed the conversations. Tuxedoed waiters, with pitchers and platters in hand, threaded their way around the tables. She wanted to step down the carpeted stairs into that blessed service to be showered with wine and meats and pastries she hadn't tasted in years, but she couldn't.

At a table for two, a hat of unruly purple feathers caught her attention. Its hefty brim hid all but the lady's jaw that moved nonstop. Her neighbors were sending over heavy-lidded glances that she didn't see, for all of her attention was on her companion. She stroked his hand with such fervor that it appeared that the man needed resuscitation. From the look of the back of his head, he was definitely in need of barber with better eyesight, Annaliese noted. Better tailor, too. The edge of his coat sleeve rode too high above the shirt cuff, while his ill-fitting coat buckled between the shoulder blades. He withdrew his hand from her petting to snap his fingers at a waiter too loudly. The neighbors rolled their eyes. The lady tossed back a glass of wine with the delicacy of a stevedore. When her arm was raised, a bosom that strained the limits of her purple dress became clear.

Annaliese's ears caught fire. She stopped jostling Georgia Ann, which prompted a scream that sliced through the dining room. All conversations ceased, all heads turned toward Annaliese. She put the baby to her shoulder to muffle her cries while she waited to see all of that face behind the purple brim. Surely not, she thought. What are the odds?

The brim swung around to reveal the painted face of Olive Washburn. Kohl-lined eyes widened and blinked at Annaliese. Her hand flew to her neck. Annaliese felt her own neck flood with heat.

Olive took a quick glance at her dining companion. His eyes were fixed on the screaming baby and the maître d' who was pacing behind Annaliese. Olive's hand slid from her neck to her collarbone and from there she turned it slightly so she could raise her index finger at Annaliese. She wiggled it in a circle. *Turn her around,* it said. Again astonished, Annaliese flipped the baby around. While gasps erupted across the dining room, Olive smiled at the little face, clearly relieved to see the chubby, rosy cheeks, clearly unguarded in this reverie and unafraid under the gaze of the woman she had wronged in so many ways. The crimson-stained lips slowly curled into a dreamy smile and the smoky eyes formed a question. Annaliese felt that it asked, *She's doing well, yes?* Annaliese nodded, suddenly flooded with forgiveness. Olive lingered on her face long enough to see that forgiveness and turned back to her companion.

39

In February, while Annaliese and Georgia Ann were in Atlanta, Herschel hammered the last lap joint of the addition to his cabin into place. A week later, Ruth delivered her baby boy. Throughout her labor, Dorothy walked the frozen grounds with her, held her hand on their way to the new Sears, Roebuck and Company bed when the midwife arrived, cried with her when the baby slid out easily somehow from those narrow hips. The midwife got his nose cleared and handed the rosy baby, crying lustily, to Herschel, as Ruth had requested. Ruth watched him marvel at their miracle, the child who was perfect head to foot, and in her eyes, a redeemer of her transgressions upon Herschel. The child was a redeemer in Samuel's view as well, another boy, finally, in the domestic mix.

By the spring of 1904, strangers no longer stared at Georgia Ann. While the February snows had stilled the slopes, while the rivers rose with the spring melt and birds flew in chevron formations toward their northern homes, Georgia Ann's scars healed. Two surgeries had knitted her lip together in an almost perfect way, save a tiny bumpout to the left of center. The palate was closed and the nose straightened. Four teeth had arrived, as had the babble that communicated all that she needed in a household with so many hands eager to give it to her. Unlike the first moments of her life that were so silent, her days were filled with the happy sounds of the household.

Annaliese came to believe that scars were a sign of having come out on the other side of something. The joy was in having survived bereavement, betrayal, a birth defect, bad business decisions, and the toxic stream of fears trickling through one's head. Wasn't there always fear, though?

On Sundays, she and Henry sat mostly in silence on his cabin porch, lost in their thoughts of the passionate moments just before and enjoying the view. Out there, Annaliese knew, some of the forests were healing, too, rising again from the resilient earth. Some of her colleagues in the industry were bending a little, some of them even coming to check out Caleb's fish hatcheries and reseeding projects, while others continued with their brutal drives. In any case, she was finding enough good in the world to be hopeful, especially about her children. She wasn't finished with them yet, but the older she got, the more she realized, as most mothers eventually do, that already the children were who they would always be. Samuel would be intuitive, charming, and confident. Her girls would be stronger still, capable and honest, curious and kind, the kind of women who would seize all opportunities for their gender that surely would be arriving in the coming decades, and even some opportunities that would be held just outside of their reach.

But the limits of reach, Annaliese had learned, was merely a matter of opinion.

Coda

August 10, 1904

Mrs. Annaliese Stregal
Stregal Brothers Lumber Company
P. O. Box 25
Pinch, Georgia

Dear Mrs. Stregal:

I hope this letter finds you and your family well. I apologize for not corresponding with you for more than a year. I am embarrassed to say that when I so casually promised that I would return to your home in a few months, I underappreciated the distances of my Georgia circuit and the difficulties of covering the mountains on a horse. Three horses, rather, though I have finally found a sound animal in my current one. Suffice to say that I have learned many things in my first year as a priest. I suppose you could have apprised me of a great deal had I had enough humility to ask.

All the while, as the months went by, I was aware that you were expecting to hear from me about what I would find in terms of the numbers of Catholics and any significant communities I might find. To my surprise, I found a sizeable community of Italians in Nelson, Georgia, all Catholics, of course. They have come to work from Italy as stonecutters in the marble mines in nearby Tate. Nelson is about eighteen miles from Canton, the town you asked me about. I'd say the Italians number about forty workers and their families.

During my two days there, I baptized seven babies and married three couples. Many of them struggle with English, so they were happy to hear Mass and the sacraments in the familiar Latin.

Before I left Nelson, several dozen men showed me the quarry. It is a vast bowl of ragged white stone being gouged out of the mountain, foot by foot. Crates of dynamite stand in towering stacks across the field they cross all day. They told me that every morning when they go there to begin their work, they pray for Mary's protection. They say, "Remember me, Mother of God." Memento mei, Mater Dei. *They tell me she has listened and protected. So, as you can see, there are numerous people in that town who speak Latin.*

Please write to me at the diocese office in Savannah, Georgia, with news of you and your children and those cathedral forests you love so dearly.

Sincerely,
Father Thurmond

Sign up for the author's newsletter at www.lindycarter.com

and stay in touch on Facebook: www.facebook.com/LindyCarterAuthor

Acknowledgements

I think any author will tell you that writing is not possible without discovery, not only of the story itself as it flows somehow through your fingers onto the page, but also of the real-life facts and events that fire up one's imagination. I couldn't have written *Annaliese, Sound and True* without the generous support of many people who helped me on that journey of discovery.

For informing me about the historical practice of law in Georgia, I would like to thank life-long friend **Robert Hein**, whose sharing of the details of his work as a Superior Court Law Clerk in the Blue Ridge Judicial Circuit (five counties in north Georgia) in the late 1970s helped me create characters and events that were realistic. For verifying information about forestry and north Georgia history, I am indebted to **Dan Roper**, publisher and editor of *Georgia Backroads Magazine*. For giving me an understanding of cleft palates and cleft lips in infants, I am grateful for the patient explanations of speech pathologist **Katy Hufnagel** of the Cleft Palate Clinical at the Medical University of South Carolina. Katy passed away in 2015. I'm so grateful that I had the chance to get to know this well-known counselor to families affected by cleft palate and other craniofacial birth defects.

For giving me insightful feedback on early versions of this book, I am indebted to my beta readers: **Marie Jo Corry, Libby Hollett, Carol Pellett, Susan Stevens**, and members of The Harvard Reading Group of

Mt. Pleasant, South Carolina: **Lisa Cornelius, Elizabeth Raub, Kari Swanson, and Karen Wager**. During one of my meetings with The Harvard Reading Group, when none of its members liked the book titles I was pitching, these ladies suggested *Annaliese, Sound and True*, which I loved immediately. Annaliese, shot through with holes like the wood known as "sound wormy", had become sound nevertheless. And true to her new self and her family.

Two women who absolutely were guiding lights during the writing and editing of this novel were **Mary Alice Monroe**, such a seasoned pro who is so generous with her writing advice and insight into the publishing industry, and **Ronlyn Domingue**, my editor. Over several rounds of reviews, Ronlyn's writing skill and valuable perspective helped me chisel my story out of the mountain of words that I sent her. Thank you, **Mary Alice**, cheerleader, and **Ronlyn**, coach.

Lindy Keane Carter
Charleston, South Carolina
2018

CPSIA information can be obtained
at www.ICGtesting.com
Printed in the USA
LVHW082242290119
605742LV00033B/716/P

9 781732 052000